The Girl of my Nightmares

Novel by

Mukesh Bhardwaj

Published By

Redgrab books Pvt. Ltd.

942, Mutthiganj, Prayagraj, 211003

www.redgrabbooks.com

contact@redgrabbooks.com

First published by Redgrab Books in 2022

Copyright © 2022 Redgrab Books Pvt. Ltd.

Copyright Text © 2022 Mukesh Bhardwaj

Printed and bound in India

Cover Design & Typesetting by Redgrab Books team

ISBN : 978-93-90944-82-8

Dedicated to the all Specially Abled people

ACKNOWLEDGEMENT

Hi all,

Writing a book is not an easy task. It takes a lot of time and courage. When you complete writing, it is not the end. It is just the beginning. After that, you have to read what you have written again and again to make the corrections. Once the first draft is ready, it comes to the editing.

Now, editing a book is poles apart from writing. Editing polishes your work so that it can be presented in front of book lovers all around the world. I want to thank Anujashree Roy, Naresh B, and Somali Dutta for helping me to improve my work and to make it the best version possible.

Finally, I want to thank my readers. It is because of you that I get to do what I love—tell stories. At last, I wish every hand which touches my book, all of your wishes come true. I love you all.

ABOUT THE AUTHOR

Mukesh Bhardwaj lives in Talwara, Punjab. He received a bachelor's degree in Computer Science and Engineering from Guru Nanak Dev University, Amritsar, Punjab. He works at Capgemini as a Software engineer.

He is a fitness enthusiast. He likes to stream movies in his free time. Not only does he love to read novels of all different genres, but he also loves to write them too. He has been writing everything from poems to short stories and now novels. He is passionate about bringing his visions to life on paper and unfolding the truth behind each character.

You can follow him on

Instagram (@ursmukeshbhardwaj)

BY THE SAME AUTHOR

The 18-Year Old Virgin

Noah's life took an unexpected turn when he overcame his inhibitions and arranged an escorting service for himself. He booked with Emmy to meet at her hotel room, but to his surprise, he found her drenched bloody body on the verge of death.

What is the story behind Emmy? Was she trying to hurt herself or were others involved? What made her get to this point in her life and why would she choose this profession?

Will Noah unveil the mask from this mystery? Or will his fate take him to a road where he never expected to go?

CONTENTS

CHAPTER 1

The Cursed Dreams

'Please don't hurt me. I never wanted anything to happen to you. I beg you. Please stop,' I shouted while sobbing.

'Shh...Shh…It is okay. It won't hurt, I promise you. I am going to bite you now, so please be still,' she spoke.

'At least open these handcuffs. They are too tight. My hands are turning bluish,' I requested.

'Shut the fuck up and let me do it. Be still now.'

'It is hurting so much. I can't take it anymore. Please stop,' I screamed in pain. Suddenly, I felt the ground under my feet shaking. My entire body absorbed the momentum from the environment and started shaking with it.

'It's okay, beta. It was just a bad dream,' I heard a female voice calling out. I tried to open my eyes, but couldn't. My body is still in a state of shock. The ceiling fan helped my sweat dry and gave a brisk feeling throughout my body.

'Pour some cold water on his face,' a man shouted.

After a few seconds, someone poured a bottle full of chilled water on my face. The water went in my nostrils. I panicked and shouted, 'What the fuck is this?'

'Everything is okay, beta — no need to curse. Try to take long breaths. You will feel better,' my mother said. With the help of my hands, I tried getting up from the bed and finally sat.

'Here, take this and wipe your face,' my father said while handing me a hand towel.

'How many times do I have to tell you not to work so hard? But you never listen. You are putting too much pressure on your brain, and it is killing you. How many times will I have to tell you to stop over-thinking?' she mumbled in an angry tone while looking at me. *It is my work, Mom. I get paid for it.* I wanted to tell her this, but I remained silent after hearing her tone. 'I don't know what that girl did to you. I am telling you Ji, she cursed our son. She died and gave this disease to our son — these cursed dreams,' mom said to my father.

'Son, please get married, I am begging you. I guarantee you that the entry of another girl into your life will heal you. Do you want me to touch your feet now?' papa said, sounding tired.

'Please papa, stop it. I have told you so many times never to say such things. If you think marriage is the cure, then fine, I will get married. You can start looking for a girl,' I spoke in a frustrated voice.

'Really beta! Are you ready to get married?' my over-excited mother asked me.

'YES. I can't take your never-ending lectures on marriage anymore. So, just stop it and start looking for a girl.'

'Thank you, beta. You have no idea how happy you made me today,' my mother said while hugging me tightly.

'Now go and take a bath. Your clothes are sweat-soaked, and they are stinking,' my father said, and they both left my room.

I am Pranav Sharma twenty-four years old one and only son of Mr. Pankaj and Mrs. Anju Sharma. If you think that our family is a little strange, then you are right. We are a bit weirder than a typical Indian family. I don't exactly know what is wrong with us, but something definitely is. For the last four years, I have been suffering from a disease known as Nightmare disorder. I know some of you might have never even heard of it, but it does exist.

It all started when I was in college after my ex-girlfriend died. Her name was Aarohi Aggarwal. Aarohi hanged herself in her hostel room with a rope made from her scarf. I never knew that she could harm herself in such a drastic way. Only if I had known that she could take such a step I would have stopped her, and she would be here with me right now. She was cheating on me with another guy from our college. Somehow, I came to know about her secret, and when I confronted her about it, she freaked out. Aarohi told me she loved me and wanted to marry me. But her betrayal broke both my heart and trust, so I left her. It was after a few days of our break-up when I heard the news of her suicide. I loved her from every inch of my body and soul, and I still do. But now, I think it was her destiny to kill herself.

The news of her suicide broke me. For a week, I locked myself up in my hostel room. My friends came to my room daily and tried to talk to me, but I refused to speak to any of them. Ultimately, one of my friends called up my parents and told them everything.

As expected, the very next day, my parents came down to my hostel and took me home with them. Moving on was an excruciating process, but I moved on. I don't know how, but I did. Since that awful day, I have had nightmares every night. My parents took me to many psychiatrists, and they all told us the same thing, that I was suffering from Nightmare disorder, and it is incurable. But my parents think that they have the cure for this problem, and that is   marriage.

For the past four years, they have been forcing me to get married. Till now, I have had somehow convinced them that I was not ready for marriage yet. But today, when my father asked if he had to touch my feet to get me to agree to the wedding, something got triggered inside me. This is it. I couldn't take it anymore. So, out of frustration, I told my parents I was ready for marriage. I don't know how I will manage everything, but if it makes my parents happy, I will get married.

CHAPTER 2

DreamShaadi.com

'Do you still have the contact number of Pandit Acharya Ji?' my mother asked our neighbor, Mrs. Sulochana Devi.

'What are you saying? Can you please speak a little louder? I think there is some problem with our landline,' Sulochana aunty yelled over the call.

'Can you give me the contact number of Pandit Acharya Ji? I am looking for a girl for Pranav. After all these years, Pranav finally agreed to get married, and I want it to happen before he changes his mind again,'

'Oh! Congratulations, Anju Ji. You must be thrilled. Yes, I have the number of Pandit Acharya Ji, but...'

'But what? Is anything wrong with Pandit Ji? Is there something you are not telling me?'

'There is something about Pandit Acharya I should tell you before you book him for marriage, but it's a bit awkward for me to talk about it.'

'Sulochana Ji, please tell me about it. We are talking about my son's marriage here. It's imperative for me.'

'Fine Anju Ji. Last year when we went to his office to book Pandit Acharya for our daughter Shivani's marriage, he tried to touch me inappropriately.'

'What are you saying, Sulochana Ji? Why have you not told anyone about it?'

'It was my daughter's marriage, and I didn't want to create unnecessary chaos. So, I kept quiet and didn't tell anyone about it till today. Anju Ji, I would suggest you not go to Pandit Acharya for the marriage. You can find a much better pandit than him in the city.'

'Yes, Sulochana Ji. After listening to what you just said, I can't even think of booking him for the marriage. Thank you for telling me the truth. We are lucky to have a caring neighbor like you.'

'Pranav is like a son to me. It was my duty to tell you the truth. We will talk later. Shivani's father is asking for a cup of tea. You know how he behaves when he doesn't get his tea.'

'Okay, Sulochana Ji. You make tea for Mr. Shubham. Again, thank you for telling me the truth about Pandit Acharya,' muttered my mother to our neighbor Sulochana aunty and finally disconnected the call.

'PRANAV...PRANAV...Pranav ke papa, where are you both?' my mother shouted from the other room. She came running to my room. My father and I were sitting in my room and talking about the marriage arrangements.

'We can't book Pandit Acharya for the marriage,' my mother said in a low tone, sounding out of breath.

'What happened? Why can't we book him?' My father and I both spoke out at the same time.

'I can't tell you that, but we can't book him for the marriage. Please try to understand.'

'So, what are we going to do now? How are we going to find a girl for Pranav? Pandit Acharya is the only famous pandit in our area. Where are we going to find another pandit from?' my father sounded worried.

'What about those television ads about the matrimonial site? What is the name of the site? The one that starts with the letter D. Umm, yes... The name is DreamShaddi.com,' my mother shouted in excitement while answering her own question.

'Yeah, I have heard about that site as well. Sonam, my close friend, found her better half on that site. She asked me to create a profile there, but I ignored her,' I said, and they both stared at my face.

'Okay, let's create a new profile for you there. I am very excited to meet my bahu. Where is your laptop?' My mother asked with her mouth wide open.

I stood up from the bed and went to the lobby to get my laptop. At this moment, I have no idea what is going to happen to me after the marriage. As they say, go with the flow, that is what I am trying to do. I picked up my laptop and went back to my room. After turning on the computer, I opened Google Chrome and typed DreamShaddi.com, and pressed enter. As soon as I did that, pictures of beautiful girls appeared on the screen. I pressed the register button in the top right corner. After registering with the Gmail account, it asked me to log in. I typed my email address and password and clicked Login.

'Why is it taking so much time? Do it fast, beta. I can't wait anymore,' my mother said, sounding ebullient.

'Almost done, mom. Now, all we have to do is fill in the characteristics of the girl we are looking for,' I told my mother. My father just sat there looking over our faces, trying to figure out what is happening.

A big popup showed up asking about the bride's characteristics. And I filled them as my mother wanted me to. While filling out the details, I realized my mother is not looking for a wife for me, but her priority is to find a daughter-in-law who is best suited for her.

After I filled out the details, some profiles of girls showed up. I opened their profiles one by one, and my parents analyzed them according to their demands.

'Not this one; look at her nose. It is too big. Not this one also. Her forehead is too short,' my mother kept rejecting them one by one. I never knew my mother could say these things about a woman in front of my father, but today she did. She rejected almost all the girls whose profile showed up as a match until she saw Kirti Aggarwal's profile picture.

'See, her eyes are both parallel to each other. The forehead and the nose are just perfect. Even her eyebrows are separately visible, and she is an investment banker. What more can we expect from our bahu, tell me? She looks like my ideal bahu.'

'Really, mother! Yes, she is pretty, but how can you say she looks like your bahu just by looking at her face?' I shouted in a low tone.

'I just know it, my son. I have a gift. Message her now,' Mom mumbled.

'What are you saying, Mom? We have not even looked at her whole profile, and you want me to text her. Are you crazy?'

'Do as I am saying. You don't know anything about girls. Look at her face. She is just perfect,' Mom said, looking at my father and gesturing to him to say something in her support.

'Just text her. Do as your mother says,' Finally, my father came out from sleep and spelled some words out of his mouth.

'Fine. I am texting her,' I said to both of them and texted Kirti. "Hey. Pranav Sharma this side". 'I have sent her the text, and now we have to wait for her reply. It can take hours or even days,' I spoke after pressing the send button.

'No. I can't wait for that long. Can't we just call her? Check if there is any contact number provided there,' my mother said.

I opened my mouth to respond to her, but at that very moment, I saw Kriti's reply on my screen.

Kirti: Hi. Kirti Aggarwal this side.

Pranav: My parents forced me to create a profile here, and after looking at your profile, they want to make you their bahu.

Kirti: Oh…They are so sweet. What about you? Didn't you like me?

Pranav: It's not like that. You are beautiful, and I did like your profile the moment I saw it.

Kirti: Thank you. You are handsome too. I like your hairstyle.

Pranav: Thanks. So, what to do now? I mean, what is the process to go further? I don't know much about this platform.

Kirti: Are you okay if I show your profile to my mother? If she likes you, then we can arrange a meeting at our home. Is it alright with you?

Pranav: Yes, sure. Go ahead and ask her. It is absolutely fine.

Kirti: Okay, wait. Let me show her your profile, and then I will get back to you.

'What are you two talking about? Are you flirting with her?' my mother asked me while looking at me with an angry face.

'No, Mom. Kirti is asking her mother to look at my profile. She said if her mother likes me, then they can arrange a meeting.'

'That is great, my son. Tell her to arrange a meeting for the coming Sunday. And ask for their address as well,' my mom spoke like a non-stop train.

'Wait, Mom. Let Kirti ask her mother first. Her mother's approval is also important. Right?'

'Whatever,' she mumbled, looking at my father's puppy face.

Kirti: Is your family comfortable meeting us on coming Sunday?

Pranav: Yes. It is fine. My parents want me to ask you about your address.

Kirti: Yes, of course. The address is necessary, obviously. I wouldn't want your family to waste time looking for our house. I will text you my address on your contact number. Is it fine?

Pranav: Yes. It is great. We are looking forward to meeting you.

Kirti: I am also excited to meet you. When you reach Kashmere Gate ISBT, just give me a call. I will send my brother Suraj to pick you.

Pranav: There is no need for that. We will book a cab from Kashmere Gate for your house.

Kirti: No, please. I insist. Suraj will pick you from Kashmere Gate. You just call me 10 minutes before reaching there.

Pranav: Fine. I will call. It was great talking to you. Looking forward to meeting you. Bye. Take Care.

Kirti: Same here. Bye. Have a safe journey.

'What happened, beta? Did Kirti's mother like you or not? Did she give her address?' my mother asked me with curiosity.

Suddenly I heard a beep sound from my phone, and on checking, it showed one unread text. It was a message from Kirti with her address — 'R-401, Ninth Floor, Connaught Place, New Delhi'.

'Yes, Mom. She just texted me her address. We will be going to meet her family this coming Sunday. They both liked me, I think so,' I hesitated.

CHAPTER 3

Lines of Hands

'Please don't do this. At least tell me why are you doing this to me? What have I done to you?' I shouted while sobbing.

'First, you tell me, how does it feel when someone defiles you? How does it feel when, with every passing second, the intensity of the pain increases? What do you think of doing when you know it is never going to stop, and the only thing you can do now is to absorb it in every inch of your body and cherish it?' she asked.

'Stop it. I can't take it anymore. Please STOP…'

'No, no. Feel the pain in every part of your body. If you try, you will start finding pleasure in the pain deep down somewhere. I also felt it when you used to hurt me.'

'What are you talking about? I don't even know you. I have never seen you in my life before.'

'That is not correct, Mr. Pranav Sharma. You know me. You know me very well. Why don't you just ask the other Pranav?'

'Wake up, Pranav beta. Did you forget we have to go to meet Kirti's family today? Wake up and take a bath,' my mother yelled from the kitchen with excitement while making breakfast.

'I am awake, mom. I am just lying on the bed with eyes closed,' I mumbled in a sleepy tone.

'I know, I know beta. Do you want me to pour a bottle of cold water on you to wake you up?' my mother shouted, taunting.

'No. I am going to take a bath. Relax, Mom,' I replied and went for a shower. The previous night was just awful. These nightmares are now killing me. I can't take them anymore. For the last few days, I have not been able to write anything. I am trying to write a perfect ending for my next novel, but even after many attempts, I am failing. My publishers are pressuring me to submit the first draft of the novel. I have told them many times to give me some extra days, but they are not ready to hear me out. I am just hoping after the marriage; these nightmares stop so that I can finally write something. It is essential for me because my writing is the sole source of income for our family. My father, Mr. Pankaj Sharma, is a retired Software Engineer. He has saved some money for emergency purposes, but except that he is broke. So, If I don't write, even for a month, it will affect our family's budget.

'Beta, what are you doing? Are you taking a bath or sleeping in there? Hurry up and come for breakfast,' my mother shouted from the kitchen.

'Coming, mother. Just five minutes,' I shouted while wearing my briefs. When I came out of the bathroom, I thought about Kirti. I tried to imagine her face in my head, but failed. I wanted to impress her, so I thought of wearing formal clothes. But when I opened my wardrobe, I found enough casual wear but not a single formal suit.

'Mom, where is my formal wear? There is not even a single suit in my wardrobe,' I shouted with frustration.

'Beta, check on your bed. I have ironed your Navy-blue suit and placed it on your bed,' mom said with a caring tone.

Let me tell you something about Navy-blue suits. If you are going on a date and want to impress your girl, wear a navy-blue suit. If you are going to someone's or say your own marriage, wear a navy-blue suit. Navy-Blue formals have their grace. Wearing them gives you confidence, charm, maturity, courage, and girls crave all these characteristics in an ideal man. I picked up the suit, gave it a look, touched it, admired it, and finally wore it with pride.

'What happened to your eyes? Why are they so red? Those cursed dreams again?' my mother asked in frustration.

'Yeah. Last night went terrible. I saw that girl in my dreams again.'

'I am telling you, that girl Aarohi did this to you. Are you listening to me? She cursed you. She cursed my son,' my mother started sobbing.

'Now, don't cry, Mom. You know I can't see you like this. Please stop crying. You told me yourself marrying another girl will cure me, so I am doing it. I am doing it for both of you. Now come here and give me a tight hug.'

'Beta, you know I can't see you in pain like this. We have never harmed anyone. I don't know why god is hurting us so much,' She spoke while sobbing.

'It's okay, Mom. Stop crying. Aren't you excited you are going to meet your daughter-in-law?'

'I am inexplicably happy, beta. When she comes to our home, she will cure you. I know she will make everything good when she comes.'

'Yes. She will. Now feed me with your hands like you used to do when I was a child, and where is papa?'

'Your papa went to get a cab. He must be coming soon,' my mother said with surety and made me take a bite of the sandwich.

Papa came after ten minutes and told us that the cab is waiting outside for us. After locking all the doors, papa finally closed the main gate, and we went down. The cab was Maruti Suzuki Swift, and both the cab and cab driver wore white clothes. We sat in the cab, and I gave Kriti's address to the driver, and he started driving.

My mother sat with me in the cab's backseat while my father sat in the front, next to the driver. He started a conversation with the driver about his job and asked him millions of unnecessary questions. I looked at my mother; her mobile phone was in her hands, and she was reading Bhagwat Geeta on it. While reading, she uttered every single word as she read them. Everyone in the cab was busy in their own little world, leaving me behind with my scary past. The entire scene of the day when Aarohi committed suicide, and I went to her hostel flashed in front of my eyes and made me relive it.

'Let me enter her room, at least for a few minutes. She was my girlfriend. It is my right to see her room,' I pleaded.

'First that girl and now you. I almost lost my job because of her, and now if I let you in, then my job will be in jeopardy. Try to understand, son. I know how you are feeling right now, but I can't let you go in that room,' said the warden of Delhi University's girl's hostel.

'No. You can't understand how I am feeling. Have you ever lost someone whom you loved more than yourself? Don't ever say you understand how I am feeling.' I started sobbing.

'Son, please stop crying. Drink this and calm down,' she said while handing me a glass of water. I gulped down the entire glass of water. 'I can let you go in there, but only for a few minutes. Are you listening to me, son?' she asked.

'Thank you. I only need a few minutes. You are doing me a huge favor. I will never forget it for my entire life,' I said, half-smiling with tears filled in my eyes.

She took the key to Aarohi's room from the cabinet and asked me to follow her. I followed her like an ant and walked right behind her. While walking, I came across Aarohi's friend Gita Mishra. She recognized me and ran towards me. She ran like a sprinter and hugged me tightly like I am her past lover, and she was meeting me after a long time.

'Where are you both going?' Gita asked me curiously while looking at both of our faces.

'I came to see Aarohi's room. Maybe she left something for me there.'

'Oh…You mean like a note?' Gita asked with a smiling face.

'Yes. Like a note or letter or maybe something else, but I can't say anything before checking her room.'

'She did leave a suicide note for you before she killed herself, but the Police took the note into their custody. I can help you to get to know what Aarohi wrote in it,' Gita whispered.

'How is it possible? I want to read it. Please help me, Gita. I am begging you.'

'Sure, but let's go to Aarohi's room first. You came here to see her room, so let's go there,' Gita muttered.

After a few minutes, we reached Aarohi's room. The Warden opened Aarohi's room and told us that we have only a few minutes to look in there. I turned the doorknob and the door opened with ease. I entered the room, and Gita followed me in, like my shadow. I was shocked to see the room completely empty. There was nothing in the room except for the wooden bed, the same bed where Aarohi used to sleep in. I walked toward the bed and sat on it. The entire atmosphere of the room haunted me. The room reminded me of Aarohi, and I started crying. Gita came close to me, patted on my shoulder, and handed me her phone. I opened my eyes to have a look at Gita's mobile phone and went into shock. It was the photo of Aarohi's suicide note, which she left for me. I started reading it while still sobbing.

'This note is only from Pranav Sharma. If someone other than him reads it, then I will haunt you for your entire life.

Hello, baby. I know you are extremely angry with me, but I have my reasons for doing what I did. Please give me a chance and hear me out. I loved you more than anything in my life, and you know it. I am pretty sure you also loved me the same way. But love is not the only thing that we girls care about. Everyone has their own needs, and I have mine too. The thing is that you were never able to satisfy me physically. Now don't take it in the wrong way; I am just telling you the truth. Everyone has two different sides; their mind dominates one, and another is overwhelmed with their physical self. You were never able to touch my physical self. So, I cheated on you with a guy from our college. I don't want to tell you his name, and it is not even important. He gave me what I wanted, and I enjoyed spending time with him, and for all that time, my physical self dominated my mind. But then I realized what I was doing was not fair to you. I wanted to tell you everything, but I am not that girl who has lots of courage. You know how I am. So, finally, the only way for me is to end my life. I can't live anymore with this lie inside me. It is eating me inside like a termite eats wood. This letter is only for you, and don't let anyone else read it except you. Love you forever to eternity.'

'Beta...Pranav beta. Wake up. Don't you have to call Kirti?' my mother said, nudging me. Her sharp, loud voice broke my chain of thoughts and brought me back to reality. Finally, I took out my phone and called Kirti, and she picked the call on the second ring.

'Hello. How are you? Have you reached Kashmere Gate ISBT? I told Suraj to go and pick you up, but he keeps on saying, let Jiju call first,' my possible future wife said in one breath without giving me a chance to answer her question.

'We will be reaching Kashmere Gate in approximately five minutes, and I am good.'

'Okay then, I am sending Suraj to pick you up. He will be there soon, and he is wearing a Red Superman t-shirt with blue jeans,' Kirti informed me nervously.

'Aah, great. Now I can identify him even in the crowd. Not many kids these days wear superman t-shirts.' I said with a bit of a laugh.

'Haha. He likes Superman, so he wears these types of t-shirts. Looking forward to meeting you and your family,' Kirti said and ended the call.

We reached Kashmere Gate ISBT in precisely five minutes, as I had told Kirti over the call. The cab driver dropped us just in front of Kashmere Gate junction, as told by my father. I am sure they must have become best friends by now, and it would not be a shock if they had shared contact numbers with each other. My father waved to the cab driver as he left, and with a blink of an eye, we lost him in the crowd as if he never existed.

I told my parents about the appearance of Kirti's brother Suraj and asked them to look for him. We stood there for a few minutes, and then I heard someone shout my name in a high-pitched voice. The voice was coming from my behind, so I turned around and tried to find the person calling me out. I saw a young boy wearing a Red Superman t-shirt whose upper half was climbing out of the sedan shouting my name while waving at us. He stopped the car in front of us and came out. His height was not more than 5.5 feet, and he was a little obese, or as we say, he comes from a healthy family. Suraj touched my parent's feet and gave me a firm handshake.

'Let's go, Jiju. Everyone is waiting for you at home,' Suraj said in an overenthusiastic tone.

My parents sat in the back seats this time, and I took the front seat next to Suraj. He was driving the Honda city with such ease that I thought that if he doesn't achieve anything in his life, his chances of becoming a cab driver are much more likely. The way Suraj drove, it took us just fifteen minutes to reach Block-R, Connaught Place.

'We have to walk from here to home. You guys follow me, please,' Suraj instructed us, and we did as told. The buildings of Block-R were such a delight for the eyes to look at. The construction of the building was looking new, or it just had a fresh coat of paint. We entered the Block-R and took an elevator to the ninth floor. When the elevator started moving, I felt a chilling effect deep down my spine, and my head started spinning. After a few seconds, the elevator door opened, and I moved out from the elevator just like the gas escapes from a coke bottle when uncapped.

'Flat number R-401 is this way, jiju, not there,' Suraj said, pointing to the right side when I accidentally started moving in the opposite direction.

I could hear a lot of voices coming from the right side, and we approached them. When we took the right turn, we saw the Aggarwal family standing there wearing fancy clothes. There I saw a woman holding a Puja plate in her hands. She was Kirti's Mother, Mrs. Madhuri Aggarwal, and was wearing a green saffron saree. She looked stunning in it. Kirti for sure got her beauty from her mother. I touched the feet of all the family members one by one, not considering their ages. Maybe Kirti was also standing in them, or maybe not, but I have likely touched the feet of my possible future wife. The Aggarwal family greeted my parents, and then they put tilak on our foreheads. Afterward, they requested us to come inside their home and took us to the Guest room. I sat on the sofa next to the bed, facing my parents. Kirti's parents, Mr. Pankaj Aggarwal and Mrs. Madhuri Aggarwal sat on the couch on my left.

'Did you people face any problem finding Suraj? I think Kirti told Pranav about the appearance of Suraj,' Mr. Pankaj Aggarwal asked my father with confidence.

'Yes. She told Pranav, and we didn't face any problem while reaching here,' my father replied.

'What do you do, Pranav beta?' Kirti's mother asked me in a very polite tone.

'I am an author, aunty. To date, I have written seven novels, out of which five were bestsellers. Currently, I am working on my eighth novel.'

'That's great, beta. We were looking for someone who is financially settled for Kriti, and see we found you. How lucky we are,' Mrs. Aggarwal praised me in a polite tone. Suddenly Mr. Aggarwal called out Kirti's name and asked her to bring tea with some snacks. Our parents started talking and left me on my own. A pretty girl wearing a red saree with a plate in her hands entered from my right side and walked towards me. At that very moment, I don't know how, but everything started moving in slow-motion for me, just as they show in the movies. Her waist moved to and fro with every step she took, and I could hear my heart started beating faster. Kirti placed the plate on the coffee table and sat next to me. I couldn't take my eyes off of her face: it would have been an insult to her beauty.

'We have made our decision, and it is positive. We liked Pranav beta a lot. He is the perfect son-in-law that we even dreamt of,' Mrs. Aggarwal said, looking at me. Listening to her, I could only smile in return.

'That is great news. Now, if the kids want to talk about anything in private, then go ahead,' my father babbled while smiling at Mrs. Aggarwal.

'Yes. Please, go ahead. You both can go to the balcony if you want to talk,' Mr. Aggarwal responded.

Kirti stood up and started walking towards the door. I followed her. She opened the door to the balcony. I tried to grab the door for her and asked for her to get into the balcony. We were just standing there with nothing to talk about. After a few moments, Kirti broke the silence and asked me about what happened to my eyes.

'It is nothing. I was just not able to get proper sleep last night,' I said while trying to cover up my eyes from her.

'If you are not comfortable talking about it, then it's okay. But please don't lie to me,' Kirti said in a flat tone.

'No. It is not like that. If I tell you the truth, I know you will not like it.'

'I always prefer truth over lies, even if it hurts,' she said while looking straight into my eyes.

'All right. I have a nightmare disorder. Every night I have nightmares in which a girl tries to hurt me. I know it might sound rubbish to you, but you wanted the truth, and here you have it.'

'Give me your hand. I want to see something,' Kirti requested.

'My hand? You want to see my hand, but what for?'

'Just show me your hand. I will explain it later,' Kirti said while asking for my hand. I gave her my hand, and she started gazing at it.

'Here, you see this. This line of your hand is crossing this line,' Kirti pointed toward my hand while showing me the crossing lines on my hand.

'So, what? They are just lines. They don't mean anything.'

'They do mean something, and these two lines I showed you they are not meant to cross.'

'Okay, what are you trying to tell me? Can you please tell me in simple words?'

'The girl, whom you see in your dreams, is a ghost. The soul of some girl possesses you.'

'What? Are you Crazy? Do you even know what you are talking about?' I shouted in disgust.

'I know how to read hands, and I know what I see. I am not making this up.'

'Let's go inside. I don't want to listen anymore about your ghosts. Our parents might get suspicious about us if we make them wait any longer,' I said with a bit of laugh, which made Kirti laugh too, and we walked towards the Guest room. When we entered the room, everyone stared at us as if they caught us red-handed. We sat on our usual seat and said nothing.

'So, do you like Pranav?' Mrs. Aggarwal asked Kirti with a bit of both excitement and curiosity. In response, Kirti moved her head as a gesture of Yes.

'Mubarakan Ji, Mubarakan. After all these years, finally, we found our bahu,' my father cheered with overexcitement. I wanted to ask them what about me? Why did they not ask me if I liked Kirti or not? Or maybe my choice does not matter. They wanted her as bahu, and that is enough for them.

'So, can we talk about further arrangements?' Mr. Aggarwal asked my father.

'In our family, there is no custom of Ring Ceremony. We believe in the marriage ceremonies directly,' my father said.

'Oh! So, let's set a date for the wedding then,' Mr. Aggarwal beamed with excitement. I looked at Kirti, and I caught her looking at me. Our eyes met, our hearts clashed, we both smiled, and our story started from here.

CHAPTER 4

Building Up Tension

'Are you missing me, baby? Tell me, how are you feeling?' I asked Kirti with excitement on the other side of the call.

'I don't know how I am feeling. Things are going too fast between us. I don't know what is happening to me, but I think I am in love,' Kirti whispered in a low voice.

'Oh really, baby? I am missing you so much. I can't wait to take you in my arms.'

'Just wait till tomorrow, baby. After that, I will be all yours. You can do whatever you want to do to me, as you please. I am very excited about tomorrow. How are the arrangements going on at your side?'

'Things are going pretty good. Everything is under control here.'

'Baby, something is happening to me. I am feeling aroused and wet down there,' she spoke with heavy breaths.

'Really? Are you feeling horny right now?'

'Yes, baby. I am so horny right now. I want you to do things to me. Come to me, my Shona. Come to your baby right now; she is craving for you.'

'Oh God, baby. Don't speak that way. It gets so difficult for me to resist you when you speak that way, and you know it.'

'Why Shona? Are you also feeling something down there?'

'Yes, and it is not just something. I am feeling like it's going to explode,' I said with a laugh. Suddenly, my father entered my room without any warning, so I had to disconnect the call as my obligation.

'Pranav beta, have you seen my reading glasses?' my father asked me while looking in my room for his glasses with semi-blinded vision.

'I saw them at the dining table, papa. And how many times do I have to tell you to knock before entering my room?' I shouted in a fed-up tone. But he completely ignored my words and left my room without saying a single word, which made me realize my value in our house. As soon as papa left, I picked up the phone, opened my WhatsApp, and started writing a text to Kirti. *'Baby, I am sorry. Papa suddenly came to my room, so I had to cut the call. I will call you at night. Now I am going out to shop for some stuff for tomorrow. Bye. Take care. Love you.'* I typed and finally pressed the send button.

It's been almost a month since we went to Kirti's house. Two days after the meeting, Kirti's parents called and told us they had met a pandit, and he had suggested that the best date for the marriage is in the coming month. We accepted the marriage date as it was the best suitable for us too. Kirti and I have been talking over the phone for almost two weeks. After talking to her, I found out that she is such a pleasant person. We understand each other just perfectly, and our choices are also quite similar. Kirti likes to read, and she told me that she has read all of my novels and loved them too. There is some sexual tension building up between us. This might be because of the phone sex which we have been trying to have for some days now. I have told her many times that she always leaves me partially satisfied, and in response, she says, 'I would take care of it when I come to your house.'

I am very excited, as finally, the day has come, and tomorrow is our wedding. All of tomorrow's arrangements are almost done, and my family can't wait to meet their bahu. I hope Kirti meets all the expectations of my family because now I can't live without her. After Aarohi, Kirti is the one girl I fell in love with, and I can't lose her at any cost. I had already accepted her as my wife even before the marriage, and I will do anything to see her happy.

CHAPTER 5

Vidaai

'Maangalyam thanthunaanaena mama jeevitha then, kanttae bathnaami supahae sanjeeva sarasa satham,' Pandit Surya Narayan chanted the mantra in a constant tone while Kirti and I just sat there in a still position trying to figure out the meaning of words he was uttering.

I looked at Kirti, but she was too focused on what Pandit Ji was doing to give me any attention. My parents sat on my left next to Kirti's parents with their hands folded in the form of namaste. Pandit Narayan told us to pour some ghee in the sacred fire after regular intervals, and we did the same as suggested. I looked around me; people sat there with their eyes closed; some talked, and others tried to use their phones secretly. Suddenly I felt a chill deep down in my spine, which made me numb, and a drop of sweat rolled from my hair, making its way all the way to the tip of my nose, and finally fell on my lap. At that moment, I remembered years ago, having a conversation with Aarohi about our marriage. Every word of our conversation was still in my head perfectly as if it had happened yesterday.

Aarohi and I were sitting in Central Park, Connaught Place, with my head in her lap, and she was moving her hand in my hair while playing with them.

'Tell me, Pranav, what if my parents do not let you marry me? What will you do then?' Aarohi curiously asked me.

'In that case, I will kidnap you from your home and take you with me somewhere where no one can find us. Then we will start our family, and we will live there happily for the rest of our lives,' I said jokingly, trying to make Aarohi laugh.

'Really? Do you think I will run away with you and will betray my family in such a cruel way?'

'Yes. If there is no other way for us to be together, then I expect you to run with me.'

'Baby, even after all these days, you have not understood me. You know I love you even more than myself, but it does not mean I will abandon my family. I can't give such pain to my parents and humiliate them.'

After listening to Aarohi's reply, no words came to my mind, and I went blank. Aarohi saw my gloomy face and bent down a little, and kissed me for the next five minutes. Every time after kissing her, I felt like someone gave me a shock of 440 volts. When her lips touched mine, our souls united, and I felt like she healed my wounds. It was the most precious moment of my life because she made me feel so complete. It was like she filled in those cracks within me, which were not even accessible to me, but somehow, she knew how to find them. Tears rolled from our eyes, and we both said it out, 'I can't live without you. I love you so much, baby.'

Suddenly I felt a pain in my arms. Again, I felt numb, which made me uneasy, and I tried to open my eyes. The pain helped, and I finally opened my eyes. Kirti was hitting me with her elbow, and Pandit Surya Narayan was staring at me. I looked at Pandit Ji, and his outstretched hand was holding a piece of wood. I grabbed the piece of wood from Pandit Ji's hand and tossed it in the fire, and Pandit Ji resumed uttering his never-ending mantras.

After attending all the ceremonies for the entire day, now it is the time for Kirti's Vidaai. Kirti was walking behind me sobbing, holding the one end of the piece of cloth whose one end was sitting on my right shoulder. I walked with baby steps while giving Kirti enough time to walk with her lehenga, whose weight is in kilograms. I never understood the logic behind girls wearing these heavyweight clothes for their marriages, or do they just like to feel uncomfortable.

After walking for a few minutes, we finally reached the departure car. It was a Jaguar XF which I had chosen. I always loved black jaguar cars, so this was the best opportunity to book it for my own wedding. I greeted all the guests and took the right seat in the back of the car. By now, Kriti started crying while hugging Mr. Aggarwal. When I looked closely, I found some tears in Kirti's father's eyes too, which he tried to control but failed. Then she hugged Mrs. Aggarwal, and this time Kirti cried with even more intensity. After greeting all the guests, Kirti sat on the seat next to me. Mr. Aggarwal closed the door and hugged Kirti again. They hugged for a moment through the window, and then Mrs. Aggarwal gestured to the driver to start the car. The driver followed the order and started driving. We looked behind from the back window and saw all the guests waving at us with love. The driver drove the car at a constant speed, and there was pin-drop silence in the car. Kirti was still sobbing with her head down, and I had nothing to say to her. But then I realized that it is my responsibility to take care of Kirti, so after a lot of thought and with some courage, I took her hand in mine and held it with a firm grip.

'Baby, you can cry as much as you want, but today is the last day I am letting you cry. From tomorrow, I will make sure you never cry,' I said with love while still holding her hand. She suddenly hugged me and after burying her head in my chest, said, 'Thank you. You are so cute.'

In half an hour we reached our home. When we were getting out of our car, another car stopped by next to ours, and my parents came out of it. My mother came straight to us and took Kirti inside the house with her, leaving me behind on my own. She wanted a bahu, and now that she found one, it is okay if she forgot her son. Papa came close to me suddenly out of the blue, he patted me on the shoulder and asked me to go inside with him.

'Beta Kirti was feeling exhausted. I let her sleep in my room so that she doesn't get disturbed. You can sleep with your father in your room,' my mother said while breaking all of my dreams for my suhagraat. As a guy, you imagine suhagraat millions of times in your mind, but every time you feel something is missing, so you imagine it again and again trying to fill the gaps. Today I was looking forward to it, but all my dreams were shattered in a second. I roamed around for a couple of minutes near my mother's room, but didn't get any chance to get a sneak-peak of my lovely wife. After many unsuccessful attempts, I collected the shattered pieces of my heart, placed them at their usual places, and went back to my room.

I turned the doorknob of my room, and the door opened with ease. When I entered inside, I found my father lying on the bed with his big tummy moving up and down slowly with every breath he took. I lay down on the bed next to him, still figuring out what just happened. The day's tiredness helped me fall asleep as soon as I lay, and I again entered the cage where I spent my long nights getting defiled by some girl who is still a stranger to me even after sharing so many nights with her in my dreams.

CHAPTER 6

The Aapshagun

'Don't stop. It feels so good, baby. Just there, nice and slow,' I replied to what she was doing to me.

'So, you are into this. How is it feeling now?' she asked with curiosity while touching me.

'It feels great, baby. Damn, you are so good. Keep doing this.'

'I will not stop even if you ask me to,' she whispered in my ears and bit it a little.

'Yes…Yes…Don't stop, Aarohi. I am almost there. I can feel it,' I shouted with no control over my body. Suddenly she stopped what she was doing, and I felt a pain in my stomach as if someone just punched me. With every passing second, the pain spread all over my body, and I yelled, 'what the fuck was that? Are you trying to kill me?' and tried to open my eyes. In my blurred vision, I saw somcone sitting next to me on the bed, staring at me. After rubbing my eyes with my hand, I got my vision back and saw Kirti looking at me furiously.

'Who is this Aarohi? Why haven't you told me anything about her yet?' Kirti asked me with seriousness.

'What? What are you talking about? What are you doing here this early?' I asked Kirti in a sleepy tone.

'I came to your room just to give you a cup of tea. I saw you sleeping, and suddenly, the thought of playing with you came to my mind. I started touching you, and unexpectedly you started responding to my touch. You wanted me to touch more, and I did. But then, you uttered Aarohi's name. Who is Aarohi? Tell me if you want to live,' Kirti asked me with a final warning.

'She is my ex-girlfriend. Now, please don't get mad at me because of this silly thing.'

'It is silly for you. It is a big deal for a girl when her husband calls some other girl's name in his dreams. Husbands get killed for this by their wives.'

'But I know you are not going to kill me. I am your baby, and you can never hurt me even a bit. Am I right, my Shona?' I asked her while making a puppy face.

'Don't baby me. I am going down to help Mummy Ji with breakfast. The tea is getting cold. Drink it if you want. Or does Mr. Pranav drink tea made only by Aarohi's hands?' Kirti taunting me. She stood up from the bed and hurried out of the room while giving me no chance to answer her.

I didn't expect today to begin in such a weird way. Now I have to find a way to soothe Kirti. Convincing a girl is quite challenging, and if that girl is your wife, you have to put in your best efforts. Sometimes silly things can destroy the relationship entirely, and I don't want that. These thoughts were running through my mind like a nonstop train when I heard someone shouting.

'Pranav beta, what are you doing in your room? If you have had your bath, then come down to have breakfast with us. Kirti beta is making sandwiches for all of us,' my mother called me out with excitement in her tone.

'I was just going to take a shower. I will be down in fifteen minutes,' I shouted, grabbing the towel from my wardrobe, and went to get a bath. After taking a bath, I changed into fresh clothes and went down for breakfast.

While walking toward the dining table, I saw Kirti making sandwiches in the kitchen. She saw me and then rolled her eyes and kept doing her work. My father saw me coming and after greeting me the good morning he offered me the seat next to him. I sat on the chair and tried to get a sneak peek of the kitchen. The dining table was at the right angle from the kitchen, making it very difficult for me to get a glimpse of my wife.

Kirti came out of the kitchen with a plate in her hand loaded with sandwiches. She took the topmost sandwich and placed it on my plate. After placing the sandwich on my plate, she came close to me and whispered in my ears, 'I made this one especially for you. It will be the best sandwich you ever had.' I opened my mouth to ask her what was going on, but she left in a hurry. I picked up the sandwich from the plate, and then I realized what Kirti meant. The upper part of the sandwich was half-cooked, and the other side was half-burnt. I hid the burnt part of the sandwich from my father, and with a smile on my face, I took a bite from my "special" sandwich. My mother came out with two cups of coffee and placed them in front of us. The coffee acted as my life-saver as I was finally able to gulp down the sandwich with its help. After eating my special sandwich made by my lovely wife, I went to my room. I wanted to complete the first draft of my novel by the end of the day, so I started working as soon as I entered my room.

'Beta today is your Mooh dikhai. All the neighbors and my friends will be coming by 3 p.m. to our house. So, make sure you get ready by then. If you need anything, then don't hesitate to ask me. I am like your mother,' my mother said to Kirti with a caring tone.

'Okay, Mummy Ji. I am just feeling a little tired after making sandwiches. I have never spent so much time in the kitchen, so everything is new for me,' Kirti said to Mom with embarrassment showing all over her face.

'I can understand Beta. There is not much work left in the kitchen. Go on and get some rest in my room. No one will disturb you in there. You will feel much better,' my mother told Kirti.

Kirti went to Mom's room and rested on her bed. After some time, she fell asleep.

'Kirti beta, are you ready or not? Wake up and get ready. Guests will be coming anytime now,' Mom shouted from the kitchen to check on Kirti. But Kirti was in such a deep sleep that she didn't hear Mom's words.

Kirti woke up precisely at 2:50 p.m. and was shocked to see the time on the clock. She couldn't believe that she had slept for approximately 3 hours. She stood up in a hurry, changed into new clothes, and put on some makeup at the last moment. After dressing up, she went down with her head and face covered with her dupatta. The whole room was filled with chirpy voices of the ladies sitting in there talking, laughing, and doing their favorite thing - gossiping. Kirti went close to the sofa quietly and sat down. My mother came close to Kirti, patted her head while caressing it, blessed her, and stood next to her.

Mrs. Sulochana Devi came close to Kirti to offer her blessings. She lifted Kirti's dupatta and went blank. For a moment, Mrs. Devi became speechless. She took a moment to speak up, and the words that came out of her mouth were, 'This is an apshagun. She is not wearing any makeup, and nor is she wearing her Mangal Sutra and Chooda.' After hearing what Mrs. Devi said, all the other ladies gathered around Kirti and tried to get a look at her face and shouted in unison, 'this is an apshagun.'

After hearing the ladies say the same thing about her bahu, my mother felt a chill down in her spine and collapsed on the floor. The room became utterly quiet, and some ladies picked her up and made her sit next to Kirti, who by then had panicked and started sobbing while looking at her Sasuma.

After hearing the noise coming from downstairs, I went down to check what was going on. When I reached downstairs, I saw Mrs. Sulochana Devi helping my mother with a glass of water.

'What happened, Mom? Is everything okay?' I asked my mother. But in return, everyone just stared at me with blank faces.

'Beta, your mother fainted, but now she is feeling better, I think,' Mrs. Sulochana Devi finally replied to my question.

Mom, are you feeling okay? Did you sleep well last night?' I asked my mother, stepping closer to her.

'It's nothing, beta. Everything is fine,' my mother spoke in a weak voice while looking at Kirti's face in disgust. I stood there for a while next to my mother, trying to figure out just what happened. All the ladies came one by one and blessed Kirti and gave her Shagun. After everyone left, my mother went to her room without speaking a single word to me. I looked at her blank face, and it was clear to me that something wrong had happened.

'What happened, Kirti? My mother looked upset,' I asked Kirti, but she too went to her room without answering me, hiding her face while sobbing. I decided not to go after her and give her some space and time to calm her mind down and went to my publisher's office for a meeting.

I came back by 8 p.m. with the hope that everything would be back to normal. When I entered the lobby, I saw my father sitting at the dining table waiting for dinner. He asked me for dinner, and I told him that I was going to my room to freshen up.

After freshening up, I came down and sat next to my father. The dinner table was quiet. No one spoke a single word while eating. My mother ate her dinner quietly, and even Kirti was eating her dinner without looking up at all.

I finally broke the silence and spoke, 'the dinner is so delicious. Who made it Mom?'

'Your wife cooked it. I helped her too,' Mom replied, taking her last bite and stood up to leave.

'Did something happen, Papa? Mom is behaving a little differently today. Did you notice it too, or is it just me?' I asked my father, who was too busy chewing his salad. After gulping his bite, he spoke, 'no beta. Everything is okay. She looks just fine to me as always.'. Papa glanced at Kirti and me while replying for a bit and went back to eating.

After dinner, I went to my room and turned on the television. I browsed through different channels and finally found something worth watching. Set Max was showing Sooryavansham for the millionth time, and I watched it like a kid as it was my first time.

Kirti came to the room approximately an hour later. She picked up her nightwear and went to the bathroom to change. I looked at her when she came out of the bathroom with my eyes wide open. She looked so sexy in the red nighty that she was wearing.

'Wow! Baby, you look so hot. Come here, my red chili,' I said to her with excitement, but she completely ignored me and lay down on the bed next to me with her back towards me.

'Baby, what's wrong? Why are you behaving like this? Are you still mad at what happened in the morning?' I asked her.

'Why do you think I am angry? Take a wild guess and let me know,' Kirti taunted me with her back still towards me. I got up from the bed and, turning towards Kirti, I said, 'Come on, get up. I want to say something to you. Baby, please come here.' She couldn't resist, and finally, she got up from the bed and came close to me.

'Give me your hand,' I said to her while asking for her hand, to which she placed her hand in mine. Holding her hand, I kneeled and kissed her hand.

'I know you are angry with me, and after what I did, you have every right to be angry too. Aarohi was my ex-lover, and she committed suicide by hanging herself in her hostel room. From that day onwards, I thought I would never love someone as I used to love her. But then you came into my life, everything changed. You made me fall in love with you, and now I cannot imagine spending a day of my life without you. I know you might feel that these are some cheesy filmy dialogues from some movie, but trust me, it's not. Every single word of what I speak is coming straight from the depth of my heart. I promise that I will always protect you from anything and everything, and I will not let anything happen to you. Just because we are married, don't take me as just your husband. Let's be friends for each other too, let's be partners, more than that, let us be each other's support system. You help me, and I will help you back. Let us lift each other together to the greatest heights. I promise I will never let my ego come in between us and destroy this beautiful relationship that we have. Baby, will you please forgive me for my silly mistake?' I stopped speaking and looked at Kirti. She was looking at me with her eyes filled with tears. She came closer to me, hugged me tightly, and started crying. Suddenly, out of surprise, she brought her face in front of me and started kissing me. All the love, the sexual tension building up for days between us, could be felt the way she kissed me. I started kissing her back. We both lost control over ourselves. I made Kirti lie down on the bed, got up on top of her, and started kissing her passionately. My hands were moving all over her body as if they had a mind of their own. We both were so aroused, so I wanted to take it one more step ahead, so I tried to slip my hand into Kirti's panties. I was about to place my hands on her vagina to feel the wetness, but she held my hand and stopped me.

I looked at her and asked, my voice sounding totally aroused, 'What happened, baby? Are you scared of doing all this?'

'No, it's nothing like that. I got my periods today. I don't want you to touch me down there in such a condition. It would feel very abominable,' she spoke innocently.

Half shocked, and half aroused words just came out of my mouth, 'what the fuck? You should have told me this earlier. If I had known, I would not have even kissed you.' I was a bit frustrated, and it was visible all over my face.

'I can help you though if you want. I don't want you to stay unfinished,' she asked me in a low tone.

'Forget it. I am not in a mood now. The moment is gone.'

'Sorry, Shona. I didn't think things would get so fired up between us. Please forgive your baby.' Kirti made a babyface and kissed me. We kissed for a few seconds, and while breaking our kiss, she spoke, 'Baby, there is something I want to talk to you about, and it is kind of important to me.'

'Yes, what is it? Tell me, I am all ears,' I spoke.

'You remember I once told you that my boss was thinking of transferring some of his employees to different cities and that my name was also in the list of possible names?'

'Yes, you told me that earlier. So, what happened?'

'Yesterday I received an email from my company, and they told me I have been transferred to Bangalore. They want me to shift to Bangalore by Monday.'

'What? Why didn't you tell me about this yesterday? What have you thought about it?'

'Baby, you were so happy yesterday, and I didn't want to spoil your mood. So, I decided to tell you about it later. I don't know what to do. Please help me.'

'Well, if there is no other option, then you should go there. I mean, your work is important to you, and I don't want to be the one to stop you.'

'Shona, I was thinking, what if you come with me to Bangalore. It will be very fun. What will I do there without you? What do you think about this idea?'

'I don't have a problem, but if my mother even gets to know about this, she will get a heart attack. I don't think she will let me go there with you.'

'Baby, I want you to come with me. Please do this for me. I will never ask anything after this. Please come to Bangalore with me.' Kirti kept on insisting. She had such a cute little face on, and I couldn't say no to her.

'Fine. I will try to talk to Mom about it. I can't promise you anything right away, but I will try my best to convince her,' I said to her while looking at the ceiling fan.

Kirti placed her head on my chest and hugged me tightly after listening to what I said. I closed my eyes while feeling the same warmth that I felt when Aarohi used to hug me in the same way, and I fell asleep.

CHAPTER 7

Urgency to Shift

'Mom, I want to talk to you about something. Please don't get angry and promise me that first, you will listen to me completely,' I said to my mother, who was busy filling my plate with another aloo paratha.

'How many times have I told you not to talk while having breakfast? It is not proper manners to speak while you are eating. It shows disrespect towards the food,' Mom said to me with a straight face.

'Tell me, what do you want to talk about?' my father said while looking at Mom, and then he rolled his eyes and looked at me.

'I have to shift to Bangalore with Kirti. It is a very urgent matter,' I said and tried not to look directly into the eyes of either of my parents and kept eating my aloo paratha.

'What are you talking about, my son? Did Kirti ask you to move to some other place? First, she embarrassed me in front of my friends, and now she is trying to take my son away from me,' she sounded angry, and her eyes were filled with tears.

'What are you talking about, Mom? When did she embarrass you? Why did you not say anything to me?' I enquired, but my mother kept on sobbing and rested her head on the dining table.

'Didn't she tell you anything about what happened yesterday? Why would she tell you? She wants you on her side,' Mom taunted me and then stared at my father.

'Will you please tell me what happened? Papa, do you know anything about it?'

'She did not wear her Mangal Sutra and Chooda in her Mooh dikhai and did not even put on any makeup. How can she forget about all of these things? What type of girl is she?' Mom shouted in rage.

'So, what Mom? Not wearing Mangal Sutra and Chooda is not the same as committing a crime. Why are you making such a fuss about it?' I asked my mother. In reply, she just looked at me in disgust.

'Don't you realize what happened? It was an apshagun.'

'Mom, how many times do I have to tell you to not believe in these things? They are just some meaningless rituals and nothing else. Believing in them does not do any good. See, even now, you are angry with your newly-wed bahu because of something so silly.'

'Beta, don't listen to her. After watching all these TV shows and doing what these pandits tell her to do, she has gone mad. And listening to these pandits, people start offering water to the sun. Even those who never watered a single plant in their entire life are also doing it. I don't know what will happen to these people,' my father said while looking at my mother, and she started sobbing even more.

'Don't cry, Mom. Nothing has happened. Don't put too much pressure on your mind. You know, when you take too much tension, your blood pressure rises,' I tried to console my sobbing mother with a caring tone.

'Why do you guys want to shift to Bangalore? Why did you think of moving in such haste?' my father questioned while chewing a bite of his aloo paratha.

'Kirti received a letter from her company. They have transferred her to Bangalore, and they want her to attend office there from the upcoming Monday.'

'Oh, okay. So, you guys do what is required. And don't worry about us. We can take care of ourselves as we are not that old yet,' Papa said, trying to make us laugh, but instead, my mother started crying even more loudly.

'Please stop crying, Mom. I will talk with Kirti and make sure nothing like this ever happens in the future. And about moving to another place, it's not like that I am leaving you both. You know I can never think about leaving you alone. We will come to meet you guys at regular intervals. Now please stop crying and here, have some water,' I said and helped her drink some water. She took a sip, and the water calmed her down a bit. Just then, Kirti came to the dining table to have breakfast.

'I am so sorry. I was washing my hair. That's why it took me longer than usual,' Kirti said while looking at me and made an apologetic face.

'It is okay, Beta. Here, have some parathas. Your mummy made these aloo parathas especially for you. She said my bahu loves aloo parathas, and she wanted to surprise you with these,' my father said to Kirti, which filled her eyes with tears.

'Mummy Ji, you didn't even forget that aloo parathas are my favorite, and look at me. I didn't even bother to apologize about yesterday's incident. What type of bahu am I?' Kirti began to sob.

'Aww...Mera bacha. Stop crying. There is nothing to be sorry about. Things like these happen. You don't have to take them seriously. They mean nothing,' my mother said to Kirti and pulled her close to give her a hug. Papa and I just looked at them with our mouths wide open in amazement. My mother has only shown us the best possible example of hypocrisy. They hugged for some time, and everything went back to normal in the blink of an eye.

'So, when are you guys leaving for Bangalore? There is a lot of packing you guys have to do if you made your mind to move,' my mother said while hiding tears in her eyes from all of us.

'I haven't checked the availability of the trains yet. But I will do it soon. It might take days for the tickets to get confirmed,' I said while chewing a bite of paratha.

'We have to leave on Friday, only then can we reach Bangalore on time. My friend Anjali Saxena has many connections in real estate. She can help us get a flat in Bangalore easily,' said Kirti with certainty.

'That is great news, Beta. Let us know if you guys need any help. If you need any money, then tell your mother-in-law, she will give it to you,' Papa said and left to meet his Yoga club friends. After finishing my lunch, I went to my room to book the train tickets. Kirti went to the kitchen with Mom to help her wash the dishes.

I opened Google Chrome on my laptop and searched for the trains from New Delhi to Bangalore. MakeMyTrip showed many suggestions, but I couldn't find the one best suitable for us. Then I came across the Bangalore Rajdhani train, which starts at 8:45 p.m. from H-NIZAMUDDIN (NZM) and drops you at KSR BENGALURU CITY JUNCTION (SBC) on 6:40 a.m. on the morning of the third day. I checked the available seat status and found 10 First class AC seats available. In a hurry, I booked two lower seats for Friday's journey and paid the bill via my Debit card. My phone made a beep sound. I received a confirmation text for the tickets I booked on my phone. When I finished booking the ticket, Kirti came to the room and asked me to book the train tickets. I showed her my phone.

After seeing the train schedule, Kirti questioned, 'Baby, this train starts from H-Nizamuddin. How are we going to reach H-Nizamuddin so late at night?'

'We can book a cab from here to H-Nizamuddin. You don't worry,' I confronted Kirti.

'Oh, that is a great baby. It's Wednesday today, and our train is on Friday. We don't have much time to do the packing, and I also have to buy some personal stuff.'

'We have two days, and that is more than enough for packing our things. Also, I am free right now, so if you want, we can go to the market to shop.'

'Yeah, that's good. We can take Mummy Ji with us too and buy something good for her and Papa Ji. I know they are extremely worried about our sudden plan of moving to a different city. The gifts will cheer them up a little.'

'That's a brilliant idea. You sure do know how to impress someone. You have a gift, my Shona,' I said to Kirti and pulled her close to me and gave her a smooch on the lips.

'What are you doing? Mummy Ji will see us. Even the door is not closed,' Kirti uttered in a worried tone. Then we went down to ask Mom to come with us to the market. She also had to buy some stuff, so she agreed to come with us. The three of us went to the market, and I knew today these ladies were going to lower my bank balance like the GDP of our country is dropping.

Chapter 8

Something-Something

At what time is the train arriving? Check on your phone. Is it going to be late?' my mother asked Kirti.

'No, the train is on time. It will be coming anytime now,' Kirti responded to her while holding the suitcase.

We were standing at the H-NIZAMUDDIN Station when I heard the loud sound of the train's horn. I stepped forward and tried to get a glimpse of the train, just when I saw the light coming from the train's headlight. The train reached the station in no time and stopped. Papa picked up the two trolley bags and got on the train.

'Mom, please take this red box. My books are in there. Hurry up, Mom. The train will not be stopping for very long,' I shouted while carrying the red suitcase and entered the train. Kirti was going in front of me, and my mother was following me with the red box.

'Hurry up, Kirti. Why are you walking so slow?' I shouted in a low voice, so the other passengers couldn't hear me.

'I am walking as fast as I can. But this suitcase is heavy,' Kirti muttered in frustration and picked up a little more pace. We reached our seat and saw papa sitting and resting on our chair like he was the passenger, not us.

'Papa, what are you doing? The train will be leaving anytime, and you are still sitting here,' I asked my father with a stare.

'I was waiting for you guys. Beta check if all of your luggage is in here or not?'

'Everything is here, I guess. We forgot nothing out there,' I said to my father in response. Just then, I heard the train give out a loud whistle.

'Okay, beta. You both kids take care of each other. And don't hesitate to ask for anything if needed. You two are everything for us,' Papa spoke in an emotional tone while hiding his eyes from us. I hugged him and touched the feet of my parents and Kirti followed me and did the same.

'Let's go, Papa. I will drop you both out,' I said, and my parents followed me out of the train. After a few seconds, the train started moving. I touched my parent's feet, greeted them, and ran to get inside the train. While I was standing at the door, I saw my parents waving at me. I waved back at them. With each passing second, the train picked up the speed, and both of them became smaller and smaller till the point they disappeared like it was platform 9 ¾ and it just sucked them inside into the world of magic.

'What are you doing here? Why did you not come to the seat?' Kirti asked while standing behind me.

'I was just looking outside. Don't you think today's weather is great?' I asked her, looking outside.

'Why are your eyes so red? Show me your face,' Kirti said to me, but I ignored her words and kept looking outside. Suddenly, she held my arms and made me turn towards her.

'Are you crying, baby? Why? What happened?' She asked in a caring tone.

'It is nothing. This is the first time I left my parents alone on their own. I am a little worried about them.'

'Aww…You are so cute, my Shona. Come here, let me give you a hug,' Kirti said and then pulled me close to her and gave a tight hug. Out of nowhere, she started kissing me, and I also kissed her back. We just stood there for a while, kissing each other.

'Baby, let's go back to our seats. I don't want someone to steal our stuff,' said Kirti.

'Please let's stay here for a while baby. Can't you see I am feeling low, and my lips need the support of yours?' I said to Kirti while staring into her eyes, pulled her close to mine, and kissed her again. After kissing for some more minutes, she finally got out of my tight grip and ran toward our seats. I followed her and went behind her.

Most of the passengers were going to sleep, except for some who were too focused on their smartphones and ignored everything around them. Kirti pulled out a blanket from her backpack, lay on the seat, and finally packed herself in that blanket.

'Baby, what about me? Where will I sleep?' I said while making a puppy face.

'Sleep in that seat of yours. We booked two seats, not one. I am not going to share my blanket with you,' Kirti said with her finger pointing to the other seat and started giggling in her unique way.

'Oh…So, you are in the mood to play. Game is on Mrs. Sharma,' I uttered and pulled the blanket off of her and laid down next to her.

'What are you doing? They made these seats only for a single passenger, not for two full-grown adults.'

'Can't you see you married a kid? I can sleep anywhere I want, and if you do not let me, then this kid is going to start crying,' I said and wrapped the sheet around us and turned towards her. Our faces were only some inches apart, and we could feel each other's warm breath. I noticed Kirti's breathing increasing with every passing second.

'What is happening to you, baby? You are getting all warmed up here.'

'I am feeling something, but.'

'But what? Tell me,' I asked.

'My periods, baby. They are still going on,' she said while making an apologetic face and then kept her head on my chest. Listening to her triggered something in my mind. I remembered that Aarohi also used to tell me the same thing whenever she was not in the mood to get physical. I felt something fishy about it but ignored it, thinking it to be just a coincidence. I pulled her face out from inside the blanket and said, 'Baby, don't ever think that being physical is all that I want from you. For me, the connection between us and the love in our relationship is more important.' Just when I said these words, Kirti started kissing me like crazy. We finally went to sleep with our lips and souls still connected.

CHAPTER 9

Raaga Buildings

'Hi, Anjali. How are you? Were you sleeping? Hope I didn't wake you up,' Kirti said to her friend Anjali Saxena on the call. I looked at my watch, and it showed 10:20 p.m. But the train's loud sound did not let us sleep. Yesterday's night was also just pathetic. And today, before going to sleep, Kirti wanted to confirm from Anjali about the status of the flat, so she called her.

'I am fine, Kirti. How are you? Are you joking, who sleeps so early? You tell me, how is your train journey going?' Anjali asked.

'I am good. You know the condition of trains in India. We could not get proper sleep last night because of these noises on the train,' Kirti muttered with frustration.

'I know, I know. Listen, there is good news for you. I found a flat for the two of you.'

'Oh! That is such splendid news. In which area is this flat? How far is it from your place?'

'Actually, there was an empty flat in our building and that also on the floor where I live. So, I talked with one of my colony's committee members and told him that my friend is looking for a flat in the neighborhood. He said you guys can come and take a look at the flat. And if you like it, it's yours. I am telling you way in advance that it is a great place to live, you will love it.'

'We will take it. I have full faith in you. I don't know how we would have managed to find a flat without you. Thank you so much. You know these days getting a flat is more difficult than winning an election.' said Kirti in excitement.

'Hahaha. That is so true. We will have so much fun. I am so excited as we are going to be neighbors. Yay! Listen, when you guys reach here, first come to my flat. You can get some rest here, and then Anuj and I will help you guys in arranging your things in your flat.

'Sure. We will do that. But first, give us the address of your building.'

'Oh, sorry! I am so excited about you moving here that I completely forgot to give you the address. I will text you the address. Is it okay?'

'That would be great. I don't know how to thank you for all this help.'

'You can do one thing. Send your husband over to my place for one night. It will make us both even,' said Anjali and then started laughing.

'Haha, so funny. I will do that. Talk to you later. Looking forward to meeting you. Bye,' Kirti said and disconnected the call.

'So, did she manage to find a place for us, or do we have to sleep on the footpath? I am really terrified of Salman Bhai, just letting you know.' I said to Kirti, trying to make her laugh.

'Shut up. Don't be silly. She found us a flat in her building itself and will be sending me the address any time now,' Kirti told me. We heard a beep coming from her smartphone. It was a text from Anjali. I took the phone from Kirti's hand and read the text which said *'Raaga Buildings, Hennur Main road, Bangalore.'* And then Kirti took her phone back from me to see the address.

'Baby, check on Google Maps how far is this address from KSR Bengaluru city junction. We will have to book a cab to reach there,' Kirti said, still looking at her smartphone's screen. I opened up Google Maps on my phone and typed KSR Bengaluru City Junction in the starting point and Raaga buildings, Hennur Main Road, Bangalore in the destination location, and pressed the search button. It showed a distance of 17 kilometers, which could be easily covered in an hour.

'Baby Raaga Building is not that far from Bengaluru City Junction. It will take a maximum of an hour to reach there,' I told Kirti.

'That is great. We have to wake up early tomorrow morning, so let's get some sleep now. You can sleep with me if you want.'

'Yesterday you wanted me to sleep in my own seat, and today you want me to sleep with you. How did you have a sudden change of heart?'

'It's nothing like that. I just thought you could enjoy yourself till you have time.'

'What? What do you mean by that?' I asked in an amazed tone.

'I mean, tomorrow we will be busy shifting and arranging all our things. So, you are not going to get much time to rest tomorrow. That's what I was trying to say,' Kirti said while wrapping her blanket around her. I laid down next to her, covered myself in the blanket too, and hugged Kirti. We were both so tired that neither of us realized when we fell asleep while talking.

'Fresh Frooti…Thanda Pani…Garam Chai…' Someone shouted in a loud voice. 'Fresh Frooti…Thanda Pani…Garam Chai…'

'Baby wake up. It is time. Wake up, baby,' Kirti was trying to wake me up. It took me some time to wake up. I opened my eyes, still half asleep, my vision still a bit blurry, and I saw Kirti all freshened up.

'When did you wake up? Why did you not wake me up earlier? What time is it now?' I mumbled in a still sleepy tone while rubbing my eyes.

'It is 6:20 a.m. right now. You can go and get freshen up right now. The bathroom is free right now. Use it till you have time,' Kirti said to me and made me go to the bathroom. I came back in ten minutes and wore my clothes and shoes. The train reached KSR Bengaluru City

Junction precisely at 6:40 a.m. We picked up our luggage and got down. I held the red box with one hand and drove a trolley with my other. Kirti followed me wearing a backpack and pushed her trolley. After getting out of the station, we went to the taxi stand. We went to many taxi drivers, but they all were charging a lot. After roaming around for some minutes, we found a taxi that asked for a genuine fare and booked it. I placed all our luggage on top of the cab, and we sat on the cab's backseat.

'Baby, open the Google Maps so that we can tell him the direction,' Kirti said to me while looking at the driver. He immediately replied to Kirti, 'no, ma'am. I have been working as a taxi driver in Bangalore for almost 20 years. I know every single road and lane in Bangalore. Google Maps is for kids, not for me.'

We both listened to him with our eyes and mouths wide open in amazement. He drove his taxi with such ease, which showed his experience, and it made us realize that he is not making it up. We reached the Raaga buildings at 7:45 a.m. Our driver helped me in taking out all our luggage from the taxi. Finally, I paid him, and he drove off and disappeared just like that.

'Baby, can you please call Anjali to pick us up? All these look similar to me, and we don't know which building she lives in,' I told Kirti while staring at the buildings. Kirti took out her smartphone and dialed Anjali's number.

'Hey Anjali, we reached the Raaga buildings, and we are confused about which building to get into. Can you come down to pick us up?'

'Oh, you guys reached so early. That's great. Wait, I am coming down,' Anjali sounded excited. We waited there looking around at our surroundings. The buildings were freshly painted with white. The structure of the buildings impressed me, and I loved our new colony. I saw a chubby girl wearing a plain purple t-shirt and pink pajamas with

Barbie prints come out of the building. She had her hair tied up in a ponytail. She looked cute, and her plumpness complimented her beauty. She came close to us and hugged Kirti.

'I thought you guys were not going to reach till afternoon. You should have called me. I would have come to pick you up from the station,' Anjali said, sounding a little tender. After Kirti, it was my turn to get a hug. Anjali came close to me, wrapped her arms around me. I could feel her breasts crushing against my chest, while she embraced me. I could feel her free breasts against me, and it suddenly made me realize that she was not wearing a bra. Her breasts felt so much more significant than Kirti's in size. I was feeling a little bit aroused by the touch of her melons and I could feel my hardness inside my trousers. Anjali finally released me from her hug. I nearly thanked God for the timing, or it would have been embarrassing for me if she felt my boner. I picked up the suitcase from the ground and held it in front of my thighs, trying to hide the bulge in my trousers.

'You both must be very tired and hungry. Come on, let's go upstairs. I will make some sandwiches for you guys,' Anjali said and walked toward her building. We followed her and got inside an elevator. She pressed the button for the fifth floor, and the elevator started going up. In a few seconds, the elevator doors opened, and we came out of it. We followed Anjali as she walked toward her flat.

'This is your flat. And that one is mine,' Anjali pointed out the two flats numbered 1120 and 1123 respectively. She started walking and stopped outside her flat. She opened the main door of her house and asked us to come inside. We went inside and placed our luggage in one corner, which we found empty.

'You guys sit there and relax, I will get you some water,' Anjali said while pointing toward a sofa in the drawing-room. She went to the kitchen, and we made ourselves comfortable on the sofa. After a while, she came out with a plate filled with sandwiches and with two glasses of water. I picked up one glass and drank the water. With every sip of water, I felt more relaxed. Anjali sat next to me. Her leg brushed against mine and I felt an enthralling sensation inside me.

'You guys must be exhausted and hungry. Have some sandwiches, and then you can sleep in my room,' Anjali said with her face focused toward Kirti's. We ate the sandwiches and went to Anjali's room to get some rest. As soon as I rested on the bed, I could feel my joints giving up. Kirti laid down next to me and wrapped her arm around me. It's been only a few minutes of our lying there when I went to sleep, and by sleep, I mean – my crazy nightmares.

CHAPTER 10

Wet Spot

'Anjali, is there hot water available in the bathroom? I am so tired and sweaty from the journey, so I feel like taking a bath,' Kirti asked Anjali while sitting on a sofa in the lobby watching the World Premiere of Life of Pi, running for the first time on the television.

'Yeah, I think I have left some. If you like some more hot water, then you can turn the geyser on. Here, take my towel and get a bath,' Anjali replied, handing a towel to Kirti. Kirti took her toiletries from her backpack and went inside the bathroom.

Kirti had been in the bathroom for some time now. It was then that Anjali decided to play with me. She got up from the sofa and came to her bedroom, where I was still asleep like a dead animal. Anjali quietly took off her slippers and climbed on the bed next to me and laid down next to me. After just lying there for some moments, she turned her back toward my side, got a little closer to me. I could feel her bottom touching my crotch. She started to wiggle her butt against me. After doing what she was doing for some time, I started getting an erection. I felt all tingly. This was all very new to me. I wrapped my arms around her and hugged her tightly. I placed my hands on her ample bosom. They were as soft as a baby's bottom. She was not wearing a bra, so it was effortless for me to squeeze them. The cologne which she was wearing was driving me crazy. I gently kissed her neck. I could hear her let out a moan. This was definitely not a regular nightmare that I kept on having. She removed her t-shirt, took my hand, and placed them on her milky white breast. This time I squeezed them a little harder and began to rub my stiffness against her soft rear and started dry humping her.

This went on for another few minutes. I was so lost in the moment, my body felt a great sense of pleasure, which I never experienced before. I could feel my fluids begin to spill in my pants. All the pressure, tension, and tiredness that was building up in my body for the past couple of days escaped from my body in the form of semen. I felt exhausted and relaxed at the same time. I was still lost in my thoughts when I heard the sound of someone's footsteps approaching me. I could hear the sound of footsteps increasing. Suddenly, someone tried to wake me, but my body was still in a state of trance, and I didn't want to get out of that zone.

'Wake up, baby. For how long have you been asleep? Did you forget that we have to move our things to our new house?' Kirti said while shaking me.

'Five more minutes, baby. Come, lie down with me,' I mumbled in a sleepy tone. Just then again, Kirti shakes me trying to wake me up. 'Baby, where did you learn to do all that, that you did to me earlier? It all felt so good,' I asked Kirti with a smile on my face, my eyes still closed.

'What are you talking about? Did you have one of your nightmares again? Wake up, Pranav. WAKE UP,' Kirti started screaming. It helped me get back to my consciousness. But still, I could only open my eyes partially. In the blurred vision, I saw Kirti standing in front of me, with her hair still wet, wearing a t-shirt and pajamas. When I tried to move into the bed, I turned in the bed and felt something wet. I realized I must have come in my briefs while having the wet dream, but whatever I felt earlier seemed so real, like I actually touched someone, who made me ejaculate.

When I came out of the bed, Kirti saw the big wet spot on my jeans and looked at me with disgust.

'What is that spot on your jeans? Did you have a wet dream? Kirti pointed at my jeans and asked me while looking straight into my eyes.

'I think I did. I don't know what happened, but it all felt pretty real and great to me, and it made me cum.'

'What? Do you even know what you are saying? I think you are still half asleep. Please get up, go to the bathroom, and freshen up. And don't forget to change these dirty jeans. What will Anjali think if she sees you in this condition?'

'Yes yes, I am going. Will you please give me a fresh pair of jeans from the trolley?'

I got up from the bed and started walking toward the bathroom. While taking the bath, I started thinking about everything that took place in the last hour, but nothing made any sense to me. After a few minutes, I heard someone knocking on the bathroom door. Thinking that it was Kirti, I opened the door without a thought but to my bewilderment, I saw Anjali standing there with a pair of undergarments and jeans in her hands. I was too shocked to react. Anjali handed me my clothes, looked at my naked lower body, and left after giving me a naughty smile. I wore my clothes and came out of the bathroom feeling a little flushed with embarrassment.

When I came out, I saw Anjali cooking lunch in the kitchen. Trying not to make eye contact with her, I walked into the drawing-room and saw Kirti sitting on the sofa watching a movie. Looking at her face, you could clearly tell that she is enjoying it also. I walked toward her in an angry mood.

'Why did Anjali come to give me my clothes? You were supposed to come,' I tried to keep my voice down and stared at her with sharp eyes.

'So, what baby. I was watching this movie, and Anjali asked me if she could give you your clothes. So, I said yes. It was not a big deal. Why are you getting all serious?'

'What the fuck Kirti! She saw me naked. I thought it was you, so I opened the door, and I was not wearing anything.'

I thought Kirti went into a shock after hearing what I just said as she didn't speak anything, or gave any expression. But then she suddenly burst into laughter. While she was laughing, the main door of the flat opened, a man entered the room and walked toward us.

'Hi. I am Anuj Singh, Anjali's Boyfriend,' he said and gave my hand a firm shake. Anjali came out of the kitchen and took over the introduction.

'Anuj, this is my friend Kirti, and this is her husband, Pranav.'

Anuj sat next to me on the sofa and Anjali went back to the kitchen. The three of us sat there and enjoyed the Life of Pi movie. Anjali came out of the kitchen after half holding a big tray filled in her hands. She placed the tray on the coffee table in front of us, and Kirti helped Anjali arrange the plates on the table. Anjali had cooked rice with curry pakora for lunch. I filled my plate with some curry pakora and rice. I took a bite and the pakora just melted in my mouth.

'This curry pakora is really very delicious Anjali. I can tell you without a doubt that this is the best curry I have ever had,' I complemented Anjali, and in reply, she again gave me a naughty smile. We all finished our lunch in the next fifteen minutes. After finishing the lunch, Kirti picked up all the dirty dishes and went to the kitchen. Anjali followed Kirti, leaving me and Anuj alone. There was pin-drop silence in the drawing-room after that left, and I had no idea how to kill this awkward silence.

'So, Pranav tell me something about you? What do you do?' Anuj asked me, trying to break the ice.

'I am a bestselling author. Till date, I have written seven novels, and five of them are bestsellers. Currently, I am working on my eighth novel,' I told Anuj, still looking at the television.

'What about you? What do you do?' I asked him just to keep the conversation going.

'I work as a Senior Software Engineer at DreamShaddi.com. I have just completed my third year in that company. It is a startup, and I am one of the co-founders.'

'That is a great man. Even I met my wife Kirti on the DreamShaddi website. I heard Software Engineers are making good money these days. These startups are paying handsome money.'

'What you are saying is only partially correct. We get an excellent salary, but we also have to work our asses off. Working from nine to five every day just sucks the life out of you.'

'Yeah, that is true. I am with you on this one.'

We continued watching the movie. After some time, Kirti and Anjali came back to the drawing-room.

'Anuj, we have to help them in moving their luggage to their flat. Are you free?' Anjali asked Anuj.

'Yeah. I am free. When are they moving?' Anuj asked.

'We can do it right now. We don't want to disturb you guys anymore,' I jumped in and replied to Anuj.

We all got up from the sofa and started picking up the luggage. I picked up the red book box, and a trolley, and started walking toward our flat. Anjali walked slowly right in front of me and entered the flat. I followed her and entered the flat. I placed the trolley next to a wall and bent down to keep the red box on the floor. When I stood up, I saw Anjali standing in front of me, looking straight at my face.

'I want to talk with you about the earlier incident.' Anjali spoke with an apologetic face.

'There is nothing to talk about. It was just an accident, so let's just forget about it,' I told Anjali and tried hard not to make eye contact with her.

'But what if I don't want to forget about it?'

'What do you mean? Do you don't want to forget about it?'

'Nothing. I am just talking nonsense. I do it sometimes. You can also see me naked some time, that way we both will be even,' said Anjali and left the room in a hurry. Kirti came inside the room after some time and asked me what happened while looking at my blank face. But I was still a bit confused to reply as my mind was still trying to figure out what Anjali just said before leaving.

CHAPTER 11

The Phone Call

'I am very thirsty. I haven't eaten or had anything to drink for the last three days. Please give me some water. I am begging you,' I tried to shout, but hardly any sound came out of my mouth. I looked at my hands and saw they turned blue because of the tight handcuffs, which were restricting the flow of blood in my hands. I tried to move my hands and free them from the handcuffs, but I had no energy left in my body.

'No, I won't do that. The only thing you deserve is to starve, rot, moan, and finally die in here. But I give you my words, I will not let you die so soon. Whenever you are on the verge of dying, I will come forward and save you, only to make you suffer again and put you in your shithole to rot. You deserve to suffer, I won't let you have an easy death,' I could hear the disgust in her voice.

'Why are you doing this to me? Please show some mercy and end my suffering. I can't take this anymore,' I cried in pain.

'Stop it, you scum. Tell me, how is your wife? Is she pretty? Do you like her? Did she do all the things that I never did for you?' the girl asked with firmness.

'How do you know about her? How do you know I got married?'

'Mr. Pranav or I say "the Other Pranav". I know everything. I have got my eyes all around you. But don't get too attached to her. I know she is going to betray you just like the others. She is going to break your heart once again. But to be honest, I think you deserve it. Now rot here in your fucking rat hole,' she shouted while leaving the cell.

'No, wait, please don't go. Please set me free. Please come back.

Help me, PLEASE,' I cried out loud. Suddenly, I heard someone's footsteps approaching me and heard someone calling my name.

'Pranav, wake up. What happened? Why are you screaming? Was it one of your nightmares again?' Kirti asked with care while trying to wake me up. I opened my eyes and saw Kirti standing in front of me.

'You are okay, Pranav. Everything is fine. Shh…Shh…Calm down. I have got you. Take deep breaths,' she said and tried to console me. My body was still in shock.

'Will you please give me some water. I am really thirsty, I need something to drink,' I asked her, still feeling exhausted. She brought me some water, and I gulped it all down.

'Are you feeling better now? What happened to you? Again, had the nightmare?'

'Yeah, I am. Today's nightmare was very different from the ones I normally get. It was more like I was living it. It felt as if I knew her, and she knows me as well. She even knows about you. She asked how my married life was.'

'Oh really! How is it possible? I know you don't believe me, but I'm pretty sure that the soul of some girl possesses you. Even the lines of your hands say the same.'

'It is all bullshit. I have told you already not to believe in these things. Aren't you getting late for your office?' I asked Kirti pointing toward the clock.

'Oh shit. I totally forgot about it. I have made some sandwiches for you and kept them on the dining table. Get up, take a bath, make some coffee, and have your breakfast. Can you do that?' Kirti said while looking at herself in the mirror with her office bag hanging around her arm. Making sure that her makeup was okay, she left the room. A few moments later I heard a click of the door closing.

I got up from the bed and went to lock the main door from inside. Then I took my undergarments, a towel and went for a bath. When I turned on the tap, only cold water came out of it. I even checked the geyser but didn't find any hot water in it. Now the only option left for me is to bathe with chilled water. I picked up the mug, filled it with cold water, and when I poured it on my body, I felt as if I saw my soul escaping my body. The cold water gave a chill deep down my spine. But when I poured three to four more mugs of water over, my body slowly adjusted to the temperature of the water. I patted my body with a towel, wore my clothes, and came out shivering. I took out a T-shirt and pajamas from my wardrobe and wore them. At this moment, I started feeling hungry.

I went to the kitchen, turned on the gas stove, and kept a kettle on top of it for boiling water. I added a spoon of Bru coffee and sugar each to the boiling water. I let the water absorb all the flavors and finally added some milk to it. I poured the coffee into a cup and went to the dining table for breakfast. Just when I reached the dining table, I saw a plate placed on the table. I flipped the cover from it and found two grilled sandwiches there. I took the sandwich in my hand, moved it closer to my mouth, and finally took a bite. It had turned a little cold but was still crunchy. While having my breakfast, I thought, what more could I ask for. I have a job that pays good money, my parents who love me more than anything, and now I have a cute and beautiful wife too. After finishing the breakfast, I thanked the higher power for the healthy and wealthy life he has given us.

I was reading the newspaper while sitting on the sofa in the drawing-room when I came across a piece of news from my own Delhi city. It said, *'A wife killed her husband for her lover. Anuradha Kohli gave Shantanu Kohli rat poison in his coffee before going to the office. When he reached his office, his colleagues witnessed his failing health and took him to the Fortis Hospital. Where Shantanu had a blood vomit, and in no time, doctors declared him dead. When interrogated, Anuradha Kohli fell into her trap and finally told the truth. She accepted cheating on her husband with her colleague and how they planned to kill Shantanu by giving him rat poison in his coffee.'* The news made me remember what the girl in my nightmares told me about Kirti. But it was hard for me to think of Kirti betraying me. We are in love, and I know she won't do such a thing to me, but still, I wasn't able to forget what the girl told me. The chain of my weird thoughts broke when I heard the landline ringing from the bedroom. I stood up and started walking toward the bedroom and finally picked it up.

'Hello. Am I speaking to Mr. Pranav Sharma?' the woman on the other side of the call asked.

'Yes. It is me. How can I help you?' I asked.

'Oh, okay. Can we talk for some time, if you are free? I hope I didn't disturb you?'

'I am free right now, but what do you want to talk to me about?'

'There is nothing in particular, I just wanted to know more about you. I don't think you have told me enough about yourself. Come on, tell me everything.'

'I am sorry, but I don't think I am obliged to tell a stranger anything about me. You are saying that I lied to you, but I don't even know you. If you know me then tell me your name, maybe then we can talk more.'

'Oh! But you and I know each other. We even met a few times, and I know all about your dirty secrets. You see, I have a diary, and I also know about the other Pranav.'

'What are you talking about? I don't know anything about any diary, or any other Pranav. Do not call me again,' I spoke furiously for the first time in my life on a call just then I heard someone knocking on the main door, and I finally hung up. Again, I heard the knock and I went to open the door. I rotated the doorknob and opened the door, and what I saw just blew my mind. Anjali was standing in front of me with only her bathrobe on. She was looking so hot that I couldn't stop staring at her cleavage. It took a lot of effort but with a bit of self-control, I shifted my eyes to her face.

'Hello, Pranav. I am sorry if I disturbed you, but I needed some help.'

'No. I was free. You know, writers don't have much work to do. Tell me how can I help you,' I said in an overexcited tone with my mouth wide open like a dog.

'Actually, the shower in our washroom is not working. I tried to turn it on, but I think it is clogged. Can you help me with that?'

'Yes, of course. Let me get my tool kit, and then we will go to your flat,' I said and went to get the toolkit, and then we went to her flat.

'What were you doing all alone? I thought you must be sleeping,' Anjali asked while walking next to me.

'I had this weirdest phone call ever before you came. I have never heard her voice in my entire life, but she was saying that I know her very well. She even said that we have met. Can you believe this?'

'OMG. This is so strange. You must beware of such calls. Don't pick up the call if she calls again. They will talk to you, make you fall in love with them, and then, they will loot you and leave you with nothing,' Anjali said as we entered her flat.

We went to Anjali's flat and I went to her washroom to take a look at the faulty shower. She opened the door of the bathroom and asked me to join. I did as told and went inside. She turned on the shower, but no water came out of it. Anjali was standing in front of me when I stepped forward to examine the shower when my left elbow touched the side of her boob. But I pretended like nothing happened to save both of us from the awkwardness. I removed the head of the shower from the base and looked inside it. There was a lot of dirt and sand accumulated inside. I cleaned the showerhead and screwed it back on the base. We were standing just below the shower when out of nowhere, Anjali turned on the shower. The water started drizzling, we both got wet. I looked at Anjali, the bathrobe clung around her body showing off her perfect curves. I could see her firm hard nipples. She noticed me looking at her bosom, smiled at me, and went outside. I followed her like a wet horny dog.

'I am sorry, Pranav. I was just checking the water. I didn't realize we would get wet. Here, take this towel and dry yourself up. I will bring you some dry clothes,' Anjali said while handing me a towel. She went to bring me some clothes and I removed all my wet clothes and started wiping my body with the towel. While I was patting myself dry with the towel, Anjali entered the room without knocking. I was shocked and immediately wrapped the towel around my waist.

'Oh shit! I am sorry. I thought you were done with that,' Anjali explained in an embarrassed tone. The way her wet bathrobe was clinging to her, was jaw-dropping. She was looking so freaking hot. I just looked at her in amazement, completely speechless.

She noticed me staring at her body and came close to me and spoke in an extremely seductive voice, looking straight into my eyes, 'What are you looking at, Pranav? I can help you with anything if you need something from me.' She was standing so close to me that I could feel her warm breaths.

'Please don't get me wrong Anjali, but I can't control myself anymore. I want to touch you, feel you, eat you and make love to you,' I said while having no control over me. It felt as if someone else was speaking these words to her through me.

'Is that so. What about your wife? Don't you love her? What will

Kirti say if she knows about us? What if I tell her about what you just said to me?'

'What about her? I don't love her. Who gives a fuck about her? We live under the same roof, and we have not had sex yet. She doesn't have to know. Her body is not even one percent as perfect as yours.'

'So, you want me to give you what Kirti doesn't give you? You want to touch my naked body, want to take me in your arms and go crazy, right? She slinked toward me.

'Yes. I can't control it anymore. I got a boner the very first time I saw you. And after that, I even had a sensual dream about you and that made me cum so hard.'

'So, you think that was a dream? Didn't you feel like you really touched someone, grabbed someone's boobs, pressed them, and cuddled with someone?'

'How do you know about that? Who told you?' I questioned.

'You are such a fool Pranav. Come here.' She took off her bathrobe and was standing there like a sex goddess. I wrapped my arms around her. We kissed hard for a long time. She took me to her bedroom and untied my towel. My towel fell to the ground, and she touched my sack, looking into my eyes, she gave me the most seductive smile. We moved to the bed and continued kissing each other. I fondled her boobs and played with her nipples. I could hear her moan, and I knew she was completely turned on.

'My hardness really wants to feel your wetness, can I enter you? I am really in the mood for fucking.' I muttered.

'Do you have a rubber? I don't want any complications,' she said with her eyes closed. I took out the condom from my wallet and wore it. I could see it in her eyes, she was aroused and in my control. I mounted her and my stick inside her and made crazy love to her. Our bodies were glistening with sweat. We both were screaming with intense pleasure. Anjali dug her nails on my back when she reached her climax, shivered, and let out a moan. After a few seconds, I came too. We stayed in the same position for some time. We fell asleep still naked, feeling completely exhausted.

CHAPTER 12

The Darkness

I was sleeping when I heard the landline ringing. I was feeling so tired that I couldn't even get up to pick the phone. And the pain in my head made it even more difficult for me to wake up. It made me feel like I just came from doing arduous labor. The landline's ring felt as if someone was drilling through the walls and I felt as if my head would explode. I couldn't comprehend what happened to me in the last few hours. I was trying to recollect my memories, but I could only remember them up to some extent. I remembered that Anjali came to ask for help with her faulty shower, and I went to her flat to fix it. But after that point, it's all blank. I can't remember what happened after that. It felt like someone had deleted the events that took place after a point from my brain. The phone continued to ring, and I didn't have any other choice but to receive it. Finally, I stood up, and while rubbing my head I went to pick the call.

'Hello. How are you?' A woman said on the other side of the call.

'Hi. Whom do you want to talk to?' I asked in a sleepy voice while rubbing my eyes and yawned.

'I called earlier, but you hung up on me. I thought you were busy, so I called again. Tell me, what were you doing?'

'What is wrong with you lady? Don't you have any other work to do, or do you just sit at home and call random strangers around?'

'But remember I told you, I am not a stranger. I know you very well. I know everything about you. If you don't believe me then you can ask me anything, and by anything, I mean your dark secrets. Come on, go ahead.'

'Listen, I don't have time to play your silly games. I already have a really bad headache. Now I am ending the call, and don't call me again, and by again, I mean never again.'

'I know what you did to Aarohi. I know that you murdered her. I know the other Pranav murdered her.' There was pin-drop silence after she completed her sentence. No words came to my mind after hearing what she just said.

'I think you are crazy. Please see a psychiatrist and have your brain checked. Do you even know what you are saying? You are saying that I killed my love, my Aarohi,' I shouted.

'Yes, Mr. Pranav. I know you murdered her, and I have proof for that. I have her diary.' Hearing the word "diary", I could feel a drop of sweat roll over my face and fall on the floor. Just like that, my entire body started sweating. I couldn't understand what was happening to me, so I ended the call and put the receiver down. I felt dizzy, and before I could understand anything, I fainted and hit my head on the floor.

In front of my eyes, I saw nothing but darkness. A figure appeared from the dark and began to walk toward me and stood in front of me. It stood there for a few seconds and then sat on the floor next to me and placed my head in her lap.

'Wake up, Pranav. Everything is okay. There is no need to get scared now. Open your eyes baby,' A girl said to me while moving her hand over my head and started caressing it. Her words helped, and I finally opened my eyes partially. With my blurry vision, I saw a girl with no head. I opened my eyes completely and saw darkness above her shoulders.

'Who are you, and what is this place? Why am I not able to move my body?' I asked her while trying to feel my body but felt nothing.

'So, now you won't even recognize my voice. I heard people say that marriage can change a person, but today I am seeing it with my own eyes.'

'Aarohi, is this you? But how is it possible? You are dead.'

'Yes, I am pretty much dead. But my soul still exists. Don't you know that they say some souls roam around even after their death if the person didn't die of natural causes? And I did kill myself, so that's not natural.'

'Why did you kill yourself, baby? Didn't you think of me at all before taking such a step? I loved you so much, and in return, all you gave me was pain, loneliness, sleepless nights. If you had told me about your affair, I would have forgiven you.' I cried out.

'Oh my god, you still don't know. You still don't know the truth. He is brilliantly smart. I give him that. For all these years, he has been making a fool out of you and keeping you in the dark.'

'What do you mean, Aarohi? Whom are you talking about? What do I not know?'

'The truth will break you, so let's not talk about that. The other Pranav, I know you are listening to us, and I want to tell you I have forgiven you. I still don't know why you did that to me, but I forgive you for everything. I just need one promise from you that you will never do the same thing to any other girl ever again, and that you will take care of Pranav.'

'The other Pranav? Who is this other Pranav? The woman who called me was also talking about the other Pranav. Tell me, who the hell is this other Pranav?'

'I can't tell you that. But I promise you, you will know everything in the future. Give it some time, and the truth will reveal itself.'

'What truth are you talking about? Please tell me. I can't live like this anymore. These nightmares are killing me from inside. Who is the girl that keeps torturing me in my dreams?' I shouted. But she didn't reply and just sat there with her lips sealed.

'That is also me, Pranav. I mean my other half who still hates you. She comes to your nightmares and haunts you to make you feel like shit. She thinks you deserve it. She hasn't forgiven you yet, but I have. I know you were a decent guy who genuinely loved me, but the other Pranav didn't. He was jealous of you. He never liked it when we spent time together.' Before she could explian more, someone poured cold water on my face.

'Wake up, Pranav. Why are you lying on the floor like this? What happened to you?' I tried opening my eyes, but the dizziness didn't let me. Again, someone poured water on my face, and this time it entered my nostrils. The water made me uneasy, and I panicked.

'Tell me more. Tell me about the truth. I can't live like this anymore. PLEASE tell me…' I cried. Just then, someone slapped me on my face with significant force. The slap helped me to get my conscience back, and I finally opened my eyes slowly. It was Kirti, sitting next to me and staring with eyes filled with tears.

'Give me some water to drink, please. I am thirsty.' She stood up in a hurry and went to the kitchen. Then she placed my head on her lap and helped me drink that water. I took some sips of it and then, with my arm, pushed the glass away. She helped me to stand up and made me sit on the sofa. I could still feel dizziness in my head, but it was bearable.

'What happened, baby? Did you faint? What is happening to you these days?' Kirti asked and started sobbing.

'Yes, I think. I am feeling much better now. Please stop crying. I can't see you like this. Baby, promise me no matter what happens, but you will never leave me,' I said and tears rolled down from my eyes while looking at Kirti's face. She gave me a tight hug.

'I promise you, baby, I will never leave you,' Kirti said while still her arms wrapped around me. We just sat there hugging and sobbing.

'Okay, stop it now. It's too much crying for today. I have not made dinner yet. Let's go out. I am starving, and I am in the mood for eating Chinese today. What do you think?' I asked.

'Okay, baby. Let me freshen up a bit,' Kirti said and went to the bathroom. She came back in five minutes, and we went out after locking the main door. As we reached the lift, it opened, and Anjali came out of it. Kirti hugged her. After Kirti, Anjali came forward to hug me and while hugging in my ears, she whispered, 'want to bang again?' I wasn't able to understand what she said to me. We entered the lift, and when Kirti was busy pressing the ground floor button, I noticed Anjali winking and giving me a flying kiss. I turned my face and looked at Kirti when the elevator door closed. I was still in shock. Kirti looked at my pale face and asked me what happened. 'Today is the weirdest day of my life,' I replied to her.

CHAPTER 13

Rajma Chawal

'Baby, last night was so amazing. The way you made me feel, I can't even explain in words. I just loved it.' I looked straight into Kirti's eyes, with my arms wrapped around her.

'Yes, baby. After all these days, we finally did it. I am feeling like a burden has been lifted off my shoulder. There was too much tension building up inside me for the last few days, but now I feel light as air,' Kirti said and planted a kiss on my lips.

'But baby, there is one thing that is making me anxious. I don't know if you thought about it or not, but it is bothering me.'

'What is it, baby? Tell me what's bothering you.'

'We didn't use a condom last night. Aren't you scared that you might get pregnant? Isn't it bothering you?' I questioned Kirti.

'So, what, Shona? We do have to plan a baby at some point in the future, so why not now? Why did you think that it would bother me? I wanted to tell you about this but didn't get time to. I have been planning for a kid for a very long time. Baby, please don't get mad, but last night I intentionally had sex with you just to get pregnant. That's why I didn't let you use it. I made you do it without a condom.'

'What the fuck are you talking about? Are you saying that you tricked me into having sex just to get you pregnant?'

'Yes, baby. But I didn't have any other choice. I want a baby badly. I wanted to discuss it with you, but I got scared thinking what if I could not convince you? So, I did what I had to.'

'How can you do such a thing? Didn't you think my decision is also important in this matter? What were you thinking, Kirti? Are you mad or what?'

'I am sorry, baby. I know I didn't think it through, but we will figure something out together. Please don't get mad at me. If you love your Shona, then forgive her.'

'I need some time to think and absorb what you just said. Aren't you getting late for your office?'

'I am, but first, promise me you will accept the baby if I get pregnant.'

'I told you, I need time to think. I can't promise you anything at the moment,' I said while shifting my eyes from her face to the ceiling fan. Kirti kept looking at my face for a few seconds and finally got up to get ready for her office. Just when she left the room, I felt panic strike me. My entire body started sweating and shivering. I tried to take long breaths, but that didn't help. I didn't know what was wrong with me. At one moment, I feel pretty normal, and the next, my whole body is drenched with sweat. I think I have to see some doctor before it gets too late. I was still tired and thinking about all these made me even more exhausted. And just like that, the goddess of sleep took over me.

'Baby, I am going to the office. Wake up and lock the main door,' Kirti whispered in my ear. But no words reached my mind as I was in slumber. 'Baby, I am leaving. Wake up. I have made breakfast and placed it on the dining table,' shouted Kirti. This time her chirpy voice went straight into my ear. Her high-pitched voice made me uneasy and finally woke me up.

'Fine. Don't bother to tell me anything from now on. Do whatever you have to do,' I taunted her and pretended to sleep with my eyes shut. She moved her face close to mine and placed a kiss on my forehead. She got up, adjusted her clothes and hair while looking in the mirror, and left for her office. I stood up when I heard Kirti leaving and walked to the main door to lock it from inside. The thoughts of what Kirti told me in the morning were still haunting me and were making my head explode. I thought it would be better to wash off these thoughts, so I went for a bath. I took a vest, a brief, a towel with me. As soon as the chilled water poured over my head, I could feel all the pores of my body opening and releasing the stress accumulated through them. The water made me feel much better and lighter. After the bath, I ate breakfast and the thought of Kirti entered my mind again. I wanted to stop thinking about it, but I felt like some part of me was not letting me. The landline rang again, and its ring triggered something inside me like someone wanted me to receive the call very desperately. I stood up and went to the bedroom to receive the call.

'Hello. Is this Mr. Pranav Sharma talking?'

'Yes, It's me. I have been thinking about you since yesterday,' I said to the woman on the other side of the call with no control over myself.

'Oh really. Why is that? If I am not wrong, then you want to know more about the diary. Right?'

'Yes. I want to know about the fucking diary. Tell me where you are calling from? I will come to your place, and we will make a deal.'

'Oh, what deal? Do you want that diary? Are you that psyched about the diary that you are ready to meet me?'

'Cut the bullshit. Just tell me what you need in exchange for that diary? Money, sex, or do you want me to kill someone?'

'So, at last, you came out from your rathole. I was thinking for how long will I have to wait to talk with you.'

'If I get to know who you are, I will kill you, you know that right? I will butcher you into small pieces and feed them to street dogs. If you have that diary, then I suppose you must have read it. And you know what I am capable of doing.'

'Yes, Mr. "the Other Pranav", I know all about your capabilities, but the thing is, I am not scared of you. You are pathetic, ugly, scum, a piece of shit that does not deserve to live in this world. And I promise you, your end is approaching you soon. Get ready to face the consequences of your doing.'

'Fuck you, bitch,' I said and ended the call. Just when I put the receiver down, I started sweating. But what shocked me the most was that when I tried to remember who I talked to and what we spoke about, I couldn't remember a thing. My mind just went blank, like an untouched piece of paper. The more I tried to think, the more it puzzled me. I felt like I lost my thoughts in a labyrinth, and they lost their way back to my mind. I sat down on the sofa, trying to calm myself when I remembered what happened last night with Anjali. I wanted to know why Anjali was behaving like that, so I stood up and went to confront her. I knocked on her door, but no one came to open it. I knocked on the door again, this time twice. I heard someone's footsteps approaching the door. After a few seconds, the sound stopped, and finally, the door opened. I saw Anjali standing in front of me in her pink nightwear. She looked so hot in that nightwear, making me want to get a look at her body. But then I remembered why I came to her place, and half-heartedly I shifted my eyes to her face.

'Anjali, I wanted to talk about yesterday. About what you said when we met outside the lift. I want to know why you said that?' I said in a flat tone with my eyes focused on her face.

'Come inside first. We will talk about it later.' Anjali asked me to come inside. I walked behind her like a dog, and she sat on the sofa.

'Come, sit next to me and tell me what you want to talk about?' she said in a flat tone with no expressions on her face while pointing at the sofa.

'Why did you say all that to me last night? And what about that winking and flying kiss?'

'Are you messing with me? If yes, then please tell me because I am also in the mood for playing games today. Tell me how you feel about role-playing?'

'I am not playing any games with you. Just tell me what I asked, and I will be on my way,' I said in a serious tone and looked straight into Anjali's eyes.

'Didn't you like spending time with me? I thought you enjoyed that day. I don't know why you are behaving like this. Did Kirti say something about me?'

'Stop it, Anjali. I know what you are trying to do here. There is nothing that can happen between us, so please stop pushing it. I love my wife more than anything. No girl can take her place in my life, not even you. Get this thing straight into your head and never do such a thing again,' I said in an angry tone and stood up to leave. Something inside was trying to stop me, but with a bit of courage, I went out.

I walked to my house and locked the door from inside. My heart was beating at a higher pace than usual, and I felt a chill deep down my spine. I sat on the sofa and started taking long breaths. It helped me relax a little, and I felt normal again. I thought about what Anjali said to me but ignored it. Maybe she is going a little mad, I thought. I looked at the coffee table and saw the "Half-Girlfriend" novel written by Chetan Bhagat there. I had been trying to read it for many days, but the daily chores didn't let me. I picked the book up and smelled the pages. Smelling them made me feel like I was standing on the road on a rainy day. Whenever I smell the pages of a book, its scent takes me to some other world. It made me feel alive. I began reading the book and after reading five chapters I felt tired and thought of taking a quick nap.

I looked at the clock, and it showed 3:30 p.m. I picked my phone, set the alarm for 6 p.m., and went to sleep in no time.

The alarm did its job and rang precisely at 6 p.m. The loud volume of the alarm woke me up. I got up, rubbing my eyes, turned off the alarm. Then I went to the bathroom and washed my face with cold water and got my senses back. I thought of cooking Rajma Chawal for dinner. I knew it was Kirti's favorite. I smiled at myself, I was supposed to be mad at Kirti but here I was thinking of cooking her favorite dish. I guess this is what love is. At one moment, you are burning red with anger, and the next, you are thinking of making the favorite dish for your loved one.

I placed the pressure cooker on the gas stove and poured one-liter water into it. After turning on the gas stove, I threw a bowl of Rajma, a spoon of salt, and turmeric in the cooker. Then closed the lid and let it cook. I washed some rice under the running water and transferred it into a pan. And put it on the other burner of the stove. Then added double the amount of water as rice in the pan and a spoonful of salt. After five whistles, I turned off the gas and let the Rajma cool down a bit before tempering. I chopped some onions, tomato, garlic, ginger, green chili and sautéed them in hot oil. The aroma of all the vegetable-filled the kitchen and made me feel alive. I cooked the vegetables for a few minutes until they were partially brown and finally transferred them to the pressure cooker and closed the lid. After removing the cover from the pan, I took out some rice with a spoon's help and pressed them with my finger. The rice was almost cooked, so I turned off the burner. With the help of a cloth, I picked up the pan and went toward the sink to remove the excess water from the rice. While I was doing that, I heard the doorbell ringing.

I went to open the door. I glanced at the clock which showed 7:30 p.m., and I thought it must be Kirti. Finally, I opened the door and there she was, standing with her eyes partially closed, and she wasn't even able to balance her body on her own. There was a man standing behind her, maybe her colleague, I guessed. He gave me a smile and after waving his hand at me, he left in hurry. Kirti was staring at me when she lost her balance and as a reflex, I moved forward to catch her and took her inside. Kirti was mumbling something in her mouth, which made no sense to me. Her mumbling was making it very difficult for me to understand her. I made her sit on the sofa and removed her shoes.

'Sit here. I made your favorite dish Rajma Chawal for dinner. Sit here still and let me get the plates.' I went to the kitchen and drained the excess water from the rice. I took out rice in two plates with Rajma over them and took them to the drawing-room. Kirti was still partially conscious and mumbling. I sat next to her and placed the plate in front of her, but she kept pushing the plate away. Out of no choice, I started feeding her with my hand. She ate some bites and again started to push the spoon away with her hand. She was making it impossible for me to make her eat, so I stopped. I ate my food and took the dirty dishes to the kitchen and washed them. When I came back, Kirti was still there, mumbling.

'Fuck you, Pranav. I hate you. You are a piece of shit,' Kirti mumbled in a broken tone. I thought it was alcohol speaking, not my Kirti. Kirti will never say things like this to me. I came close to her and tried to get her to stand, but she just sat there still. Suddenly, out of nowhere, she spits on my face. Her spit went into my right eye, which made me uneasy. Looking at my face covered with her saliva, Kirti began to laugh hysterically.

'What the fuck is wrong with you, Kirti? Stop it now. Enough is Enough,' I shouted in an angry tone, looking straight at her.

'Fuck you, Pranav. I hope you die. I hate you.' She kept mumbling in a broken tone. I lifted her and took her to the bedroom and put her on the bed. Kirti went to sleep as soon as she laid on the bed. I wrapped a bed sheet around her and lay next to her, still looking at her face. I was trying to figure out why was she behaving like that. This is the first time I heard her curse, and that too to me. It was very unexpected. With so many things happening in my life, I feel like I have lost my grasp over it. I also started doubting whether Kirti even loves me or not? Kirti was still mumbling in sleep and looking at her like this was killing me. I closed my eyes and tried to get some sleep. But Kirti's mumbling didn't let me. Finally, when she stopped, the darkness appeared around my eyes and freed me from the pain that Kirti gave me today.

CHAPTER 14

The Love Birds

'Beta, stop crying and tell me what happened. There is no problem in this world without a cure,' Mom said to me with a caring tone over the call.

'What do I tell you Mom. My entire life is a joke. I don't want to live anymore. If it is my fate to suffer all these things, then why can't God just take my life away and get over with it,' I sobbed.

'No beta. Zor ki padegi ek phirse esa bola to. I will slap you if you say it once again. Don't say such things. Tell me what has happened, beta. Did something happen to Kirti? Is the baby okay?'

'How will I know if she is okay or not? She won't even talk to me these days. We are living under the same hood, like strangers. I don't know what happened to her, but she has changed. It's been one month since we came to know she was pregnant, and from then on, her behavior has changed. She treats me like a servant who cooks for her and takes care of the house when she goes out. For her, I am a part-time husband and full-time servant, and I know that when the baby is born, she will promote me to a full-time servant. Mom, she is making my life hell.'

'Oh, beta. Girls of this generation don't know how to behave with their husbands. Didn't you tell her how you are feeling yet?'

'No, I haven't. I don't even get time to talk to her anymore. She comes home drunk most of the time. A few days back, a man came to drop her. I am telling you Mom, that she doesn't love me anymore or has she ever done it.'

'Don't worry, Beta. I am coming to Bangalore and I will teach her how to respect her husband. When she gets slapped, she will automatically get back to her senses. You book two train tickets for us and stop worrying about Kirti and focus on your novel writing.'

'Mom, you know I am strictly against violence. And you don't even know Kirti's true face. If you even push her, she will go to the police and tell them she faces domestic violence at home. She has become that cruel.'

'You don't worry, beta. I know how to handle girls like her. You just book tickets for us. We will try to get there as soon as possible.'

'Fine, Mom. I will book the tickets right after this call and send them to you. I love you. Take care.' Talking to my mother made my heart feel a little lighter. I was carrying too much inside me for many days, and it was eating me day by day. I don't feel any shame in admitting that I was feeling a little depressed these days. And why wouldn't I feel like that? My whole marriage is on the verge of blowing apart into pieces, and that too in just one month. I don't know why Kirti is behaving like a maniac. At first, I thought she just had mood swings which are pretty typical during pregnancy, but I was wrong. There must be some other reason behind her impudent behavior. I have often told her that drinking is not suitable for the baby, but she wouldn't listen to me. She ignores me like I am some dog who just barks from morning till night. She curses me when she is drunk and these days even when she is sober. I started praying and asked God to put some sense into her, but I think he is not listening to me, and why would he listen. Earlier, I never prayed in my life. Not even a single time. He doesn't know me, so why would he listen to a stranger? I was hypnotized in my thoughts when I heard the knock on the door. While trying to put the brake on the train of my thoughts, I stood up and went to open the door. It was Anjali standing out there in a plain white top and blue denim. We stared at each other for a few seconds and said nothing. It just looked like we had lost something, and now we were searching it in each of our eyes.

'How are you, Pranav? I know you told me that we could not talk to each other anymore, but I couldn't control myself today and came to meet you. The only thing on my mind these days is you. I don't know what is wrong with me.' Hearing her words made my mind blank, and I just stood there looking at her with my lips sealed. Anjali started speaking again, 'Pranav, I think I have feelings for you. Maybe I am in love with you.' When she completed her sentence, I walked back inside without uttering even a word and left the door wide open. Anjali followed me back inside and sat on the sofa next to me. We just sat there with our lips sealed like we had taken a vow of silence. At last, Anjali broke the silence and started the conversation.

'Please Pranav, say something. If you do not have any feelings for me, then just let me know. I just want the truth, nothing else,' Anjali said while making a puppy face and wanted an answer in reply. Instead of answering her, I opened my laptop and turned it ON. I went on the MakeMyTrip website. In the history section, I saw our old tickets which we had booked a month back. After surfing here and there on the site, I booked two tickets for the Bangalore Rajdhani train. Just after making the payment, my smartphone made a sound. Upon checking, I saw a confirmation text message of the ticket. Anjali just sat there and looked at me with perplexity.

'What are you doing, Pranav? I am asking something, but you are too busy with your laptop. If it is going to be like this, then I am leaving,' She spoke in a serious tone and glared at me. But I still didn't say a word. She stood up in disappointment and started walking toward the door.

'My parents are coming. I was booking the train ticket for them,' I shouted while concealing my eyes from Anjali's. She turned around and looked at my face.

'Oh! Why didn't you tell me earlier? When are they coming?'

Anjali questioned.

'The train is on Thursday. They will reach Bangalore by Saturday,' I said while looking down.

'Pranav, why are you not looking at me? PRANAV, look at me.' She walked toward me and sat next to me. But I ignored every word which she spoke and was still looking at the floor. She lifted my chin and made me look at her. Tears rolled out of my eyes and looking at me in such a condition she got worried.

'Why are you crying, Pravan? What happened? Please tell me? Is Kirti okay?' Anjali asked in a worried tone.

'Yes, she is perfectly fine. It is me who is not okay.' I sobbed.

'What happened to you? Is everything okay between the two of you?'

'Nothing is okay between us. Kirti's behavior has changed over the past month. I can't bear the pain she is giving me. Anjali, I can't take it anymore.' I started crying. Looking at me like this, Anjali moved closer to me and wrapped her arms around me, and in response, I hugged her tightly. We sat there on the sofa for a few minutes, and Anjali consoled me. Just then, the door opened, and Kirti entered the room.

'Oh my god. What an emotional moment! Let me capture it. You two lovebirds can carry on,' Kirti said in a sarcastic tone and took her phone out. The sudden arrival of Kirti made Anjali uncomfortable, and she stood up to leave.

'Stop it, Kirti. Enough is enough. Anjali came just a few minutes back. She wanted to meet you, but you were not here, so we started talking, and I told her how you were behaving these days. I told her your reality,' I shouted.

'Just shut up. I don't give a fuck about what you think of me. I don't have any problem if you guys want to have an affair. Do whatever you want, but leave me alone,' Kirti said in disgust and went to the bedroom.

'Did you see Anjali, how she behaves? Now you tell me what I should do with her. These can't just be mood swings due to pregnancy. Something is seriously wrong with her,' I said while looking Anjali in the eyes.

'Everything will be fine. Give her some time. Meet me tomorrow at my place. We will figure something out,' said Anjali and left, leaving me behind, alone with Kirti.

'So, are you guys going on a date? I am so happy for you two. I give you both my blessing?' Kirti taunted me, coming out from the bedroom.

'What is going on with you, Kirti? You are crossing all the limits day by day. You have forgotten how to speak to others. Why are you doing all this? Is it something I did? If yes, then please tell me. Your behavior is not good for the baby's health. I am begging you, Kirti, to stop it. Please stop these taunts,' I cried out. Losing control over my body, I collapsed on the floor. I lay there sobbing and Kirti went back to the bedroom. Tears burst out of my eyes as water flows down from the mountain. I somehow picked myself up, sat on the sofa, and picked up my phone. I opened my mother's chat and sent her train tickets. I sent a text along with the tickets saying, *'Come as soon as possible, Mom. Your bacha needs you.'* And pressed the send button and shouted in broken words, 'I need you, Mom. Your son needs you. Come fast.'

CHAPTER 15

The Birthday Surprise

'Mom, why has the train not reached yet? According to the schedule, it was supposed to reach here by 6:40 a.m. Is it running late?' I asked my mother on the other side of the call. I was standing at the KSR Bengaluru City junction for the past half hour, but there was no trace of the train.

'Yes Beta, it is thirty-five minutes late. We will be reaching the station in five minutes. I will call you when we get there,' Mom replied.

'Alright. Call me when you reach. I will wait for you both,' I said and finally hung up. I looked around me and found very few people at the station. They were in groups, talking, and I could only see their lips moving from such a distance where I was standing. After a few minutes, a horn made a loud sound, the gesture of a train's arrival. I stepped forward to get a good glance at the train and saw an engine painted in red approaching the station at such a fast pace. Finally, the train came to a halt and hundreds of people started moving in and out of the train in a hurry as if they were late for their important work. I looked all around me but found only unknown faces. Some of them were dark-complexioned like chocolate, and some were white like butter. The more I studied their faces, the more they looked similar to me. At last, they all were human. Just then, my phone rang and broke my ongoing research on Physiognomy. On the third ring, I picked the call. 'Beta, where are you? We can't see you anywhere?' Mom asked over the call.

'I saw you, Mom. I am waving at you. Look on your right-hand side,' I said while waving in my parents' direction, and ended the call.

She took a few seconds to find me in the crowd. I walked toward them. My Mom looked at me with care, like she was looking at her son for the first time. As soon as I reached them, Mom hugged me tightly with affection. That hug made me feel the warmth that I had been missing for the past few days. Out of nowhere, tears started rolling out of my eyes. I tried to control them, but the more I tried to stop them, the more they flowed.

'Everything is okay Beta — no need to worry about anything anymore. I have arrived now. Stop it, Pranav. Big boys don't cry like this,' she said, consoling me and patted me on my back. My father just stood there looking at me, sobbing like a kid without uttering a word. I looked at him and saw that his eyes were a little wet.

'These hugs are only reserved for your mother? What about me? I think there is some contribution of mine also in your existence,' Papa said and looked at me. When he completed the sentence, I gave him a firm hug.

'Let's go now. People are staring and laughing at our family reunion. We can do this later,' Papa said, and we started walking toward the taxi stand. After reaching the taxi stand, I began to look for the taxi. After a tedious search, I found one who was asking for a genuine fare and booked it. The taxi driver helped me place the luggage on the roof of the taxi. I sat in the front seat, my parents took the back seat, and Papa gestured to the driver to drive. In no time, the taxi picked the speed from 0 to 50 km/s and went like the wind.

We reached the Raaga building in forty minutes, which did not shock me after looking at the way with which the driver drove the taxi. As soon as I paid him, he started the car and drove it like a Formula1 driver. Finally, the cab took the takeoff, and we lost sight of the vehicle. I picked up the bags and started walking inside the building, and my parents followed me. It's been a few seconds of standing there when the elevator's door opened, and we entered inside with the luggage. With a blink of an eye, the elevator reached the fifth floor, and finally, the door opened. 'Mom, this way,' I said to my mother, and they again began to walk beside me like my shadow.

'This is our flat. It is not that big, but it works for both of us,' I said while pointing toward our flat. We walked to it, and I knocked on the door. Even after knocking two times, Kirti didn't open the door. With frustration, I started banging my fist on the door. Our neighbors came out to see what was happening outside. Kirti finally opened the door. She saw us standing there and gave us a disgusting, frustrated look. She went inside, rolling her eyes, without greeting my parents.

'This is how she behaves all the time, Mom. She is forgetting all her manner's day by day. Greeting someone with namaste will not make her small,' I mumbled in rage and went inside. After placing my parent's luggage in the storeroom, I went to the kitchen to make some tea. It took me only five minutes to make the tea. I poured the tea into three cups, placed them on a tray with some biscuits, and took it outside.

'You are getting good at making tea. This tea is quite good. Both tea powder and sugar are balancing each other and bringing out their perfect taste.' Papa praised me with a smile. In reply, I didn't say anything, instead just smiled at him and drank my tea with small sips. Just then, Kirti came out of the bedroom, all dressed up while carrying a big fluffy handbag around her arm. She was wearing a magenta-colored saree with a backless blouse. She looked pretty hot in that dress. All of us just looked at her in amazement without mouths wide open.

'Kirti beta, don't you think the back of your saree is too short? I mean, your whole back is visible. Don't you feel uncomfortable wearing this?' Mom questioned Kirti.

'Not at all, this is fashion. Oh, I am sorry. I forgot what you know about fashion. You are too old to wear these types of dresses. You only wear your Salwar Kameez. They suit your old age,' Kirti said in a sarcastic tone and rolled her eyes again.

'Shut up Kirti. Show some respect. They are your in-laws. And I think Mom is right, your blouse is too short from the back. Wear something else. And where are you going on Sunday, all dressed up? What is in your bag?' I asked Kirti with a serious face.

'No. I like this, and I am going to wear this only. You are highly mistaken if you think I will do whatever you say. You are not my boss, so don't pretend like one. I am going to a party at my friend's place and I will return by 6 p.m. so don't try to call me,' Kirti said and left the house in a hurry. I stood up, burning in anger, and was going after her, but my father held my wrist and stopped me.

'Let her go, beta. No need to go after her. She is not herself right now. Whatever you do, will only worsen the situation. Let her go,' Papa said and made me sit on the sofa.

'Mom, do you still think you can talk some sense into her? Because I don't think it is possible. Her behavior is getting worse as the days are passing,' I said in a frustrated tone.

'We can't just give up on her. After all, she is our bahu. People make mistakes, but it doesn't mean we give up on them. I know if we all work together and find some way, she will change. She will change for good,' said Mom and sighed.

'Fine. I am ready to give it a try for the last time. Mom, listen, tomorrow is Kirti's birthday. I was thinking of giving her something good. Maybe that will trigger something in her. Maybe, it will cure her spoiled mind.'

'That is a great idea, Pranav. What are you thinking of gifting her? What does she like?'

'She once told me that she loves dogs. So, I was thinking of adopting one.' Just when I uttered the word "dogs" I saw my father's facial expressions change.

'No. You know I don't like pets. I will not allow any dog around me. If you're really thinking of getting a puppy for Kirti, then I am leaving for Delhi right now.'

'Please, you don't start now. It is just a puppy, not a lion. You will like it, I promise. Beta, where you're going to adopt a dog in such a short time, as you mentioned, tomorrow is her birthday,' asked Mom worryingly.

'No need to worry about that, Mom. I have already contacted the Malhotra Pet store. I have fixed an appointment with them for today at around 10 a.m. They said some new breeds of dogs came in yesterday.'

'Oh, that is great, Beta. You should go now if you are meeting them at 10 a.m. Otherwise, the traffic will make you late for the meeting,' said Mom while looking at the clock, which showed 9 a.m.

'Okay, I will go. You both make yourself at home. Rest for a bit. You guys must be tired,' I said and went to my room to get changed. After changing into fresh clothes, I left for the Malhotra Pet store to get a puppy for Kirti. In the lift, I started thinking about the name of the dog. Just then, Kirti's face came in front of my eyes. It suddenly struck my head that it would again create a scene if I choose to name the dog on my own, and I wanted to avoid that at any cost. The elevator reached the ground floor and opened. I went directly to the colony's parking lot and waited for Anjali. She was supposed to come down by 9:15 a.m., but there was no trace of her. Finally, I gave her a call.

'Where are you, Anjali? I told you to be here at 9:15 sharp. Did you forget about our plan?' I asked in an annoyed tone to Anjali while looking around the parking lot.

'Just give me two minutes. I am locking the main door. Coming soon,' said Anjali in an Ebullient tone and hung up. After a few seconds,

I saw Anjali literally sprinting out of the building, and stopped in front of me.

'Take it easy, girl. Why were you running like a mad person? We are not that late.' I could tell by looking at her face that she was out of breath. She inhaled long breaths for a few seconds, which helped to calm and regain her consciousness.

'I am fine. Let's go. I am sorry I made you wait.'

'Where have you parked your Scotty?' I asked Anjali while looking at the parked vehicles around us.

'There it is. I always park my Scotty there.' She pointed at a Scotty and started walking toward it. I followed her. After sitting on the Scotty, she wore her helmet. She adjusted it on her head, and when the helmet recognized its owner, it fit her perfectly.

'What are you waiting for? Aren't you getting late for your meeting now?' Anjali said while mocking me. Listening to her, I sat on the back seat of the Scotty, and she started driving. We reached Malhotra Pet store in forty minutes. Anjali parked her Scotty outside the shop, and we went inside. We could hear the voices of animals as soon as we were inside the shop. A man saw us entering and walked toward us.

'Hello Sir. How may I help you?' The man humbly asked us and folded his hands in the form of namaste.

'Hi. I am Pranav Sharma. I have an appointment with Mr. Malhotra. I had contacted him earlier regarding buying a puppy, and he asked me to come this morning.'

'Yes Sir. Mr. Malhotra told me about you. He is in his office. You can meet him there,' the man said while pointing in the direction of a small room and left. We walked toward the small room. Anjali knocked on the door, but no one came out. I tried pushing the door, and it made a loud sound that echoed inside the whole shop.

'Hello, I am looking for Mr. Malhotra, the owner of the store. I had an appointment and was supposed to meet him at 10 a.m.'

'So, you are Mr. Pranav? You are looking for a puppy to adopt?' he said while giving an ear-to-ear smile.

'Yes. I am. It's a gift for my wife for her birthday.'

'Please have a seat. I am Arjun Malhotra, the sole owner of this Malhotra pet store,' said Mr. Malhotra while shaking my hand. He requested us to come inside generously. With small steps, I entered inside and sat on a chain. Anjali took the seat next to me. Mr. Malhotra sat in front of us in his big office chair. He picked his phone, took a glance at it. God knows what he saw, but it made him smile. While smiling, he asked, 'What would you guys have? Tea? Coffee? Coca-Cola?'

'Nothing. We just came for the puppy,' said Anjali in a resentful tone and stared at Mr. Malhotra.

'Fine. Let's talk business, then. So, Mr. Pranav, what type of dog are you looking for?' asked Mr. Malhotra while rolling his eyes on Anjali and now focused them on me.

'A cute one. My wife likes cute dogs. Cuteness is our priority,' I said, looking straight into Mr. Malhotra's eyes.

'Oh, a cute one. Let me think,' he said while scratching his head. 'I think a Siberian Husky will suit you. They are really cute as that's what you are looking for.' said Mr. Malhotra with a smile.

'Do you have any Husky in the store at the moment? It's my wife's birthday tomorrow. So, I need to adopt the dog by today itself.'

'Of course, we have them. Come with me,' he said and walked out of the office. We followed him and went to another room. As soon as we entered, the dogs started howling. We just walked behind him as told, and suddenly, he stopped in front of one of the cages. After unlocking it, he put his hand inside the cage. A small ball of fur came out of the cage running. It started roaming in the room in zigzag directions. With some effort, Mr. Malhotra caught the dog and showed it to us. It had white with black patches here and there on his body.

'Now tell me, isn't he cute?' Mr. Malhotra asked and looked at our faces with excitement. I was about to give him a reply when I felt something over my legs. I looked down and saw a little puppy with light brown color fur licking my shoes. I picked it up and placed it in my arms. As soon as I picked her, she made herself comfortable in my arms and made the cutest howl.

'Which breed is this one? I think she likes me,' I said while looking at the puppy licking my finger.

'That is a Golden Retriever. It is one of the best breeds of dogs out there in the market. Isn't she adorable? She is feeling comfortable with you, I suppose.'

'We will take this one,' said Anjali with surety in her tone.

'Okay, great. It will cost you twelve thousand rupees. And as our ongoing offer, we are giving our first-time customers a deal in which one month's dog food just is free.'

'We will take her. It's a deal,' I said and shook Mr. Malhotra's hand. After paying him, he handed us a bag of pedigree, weighing almost 10 kilograms. I gave the puppy to Anjali, picked up the pedigree bag, and we walked out of the store. I drove back to the home while Anjali sat in the back seat holding the puppy. The puppy kept on howling the entire way. We reached our building in thirty minutes of driving.

'Anjali, can you keep her in your house for today? I don't want Kirti to see her yet. I will come tomorrow and take her with me,' I asked Kirti.

'Sure. It's not a problem. Anything for you,' said Anjali, and we walked inside the building. Anjali went to her flat and left me alone with the bag of pedigree. Dragging it along with me, I knocked on our flat's door. When Mom opened the door, I went inside and placed the bag in an empty corner.

'Where is the dog? Did he run away?' Mom asked in a surprised tone, looking at me empty-handed.

'No Mom. It's she, not he. And she didn't run away. I gave her to our neighbor, Anjali, for today. I will go to Anjali's home tomorrow to get her,' I said while resting on the sofa.

'Okay. Which breed did you get? What color is she?' Mom said and sat next to me on the sofa.

'She is a Golden Retriever and brown in color. I hope Kirti likes her. This is my last chance to get her back,' I laid my head in my mother's lap, and she started to move her hand through my hair as Aarohi used to do. Her touch reminded me of all the good memories I had with Aarohi. The nostalgia took over me and tears came out of my eyes, which made me sleep.

CHAPTER 16

The Disappearance

'What happened to you? Are you thirsty? Or are you hungry?' She was sitting on the chair in front of me. I opened my mouth to speak, but no words came out of it. 'Speak up, you scum,' she said while kicking on my face with her foot.

'I need water. Give me some water, please. I am dying here. Show some pity.' I laid there on the floor, unable to keep my eyes shut.

'I got to know that you had a talk with Aarohi. What did you two talk about? Did you ask for her help? Are you two planning to run out from here?' She questioned and kept kicking me on my head until blood began to flow.

'Give me some water. I am dying. Please, help me,' I uttered with no control over my body. Hearing me, she stood up and kicked me in my stomach. The kick was so hard that blood spluttered out of my mouth.

'Listen, you scum. If you talk to Aarohi one more time, then I will kill her. I don't know how can she forget what you did to us. She may have forgiven you, but I will never forgive you, not until my last breath. You have to pay for your doings. Karma is a bitch, and you will be my bitch till your last breath. I hope you get this thing in your head.' She kicked me in my head and got up to leave the cage. With some courage, I opened my eyes to look at her. But I only saw a girl walking with no head. There was just darkness over her shoulders.

'Don't go. HELP ME PLEASE...' I cried out loud.

'Pranav beta, are you okay? Why are you screaming? Are you having that cursed nightmare again?' a woman shouted while shaking me on the sofa. 'Wake up, beta. Wake up.' The high-pitched voice stung in my ears and made me uneasy. The shaking helped, and I opened my eyes.

'What happened? Why are you shouting?' I asked my mother.

'You were screaming in your dream. Again, had that cursed dream?' Mom asked in a worrying tone.

'Yes. I still get these nightmares. They didn't stop even after getting married. They are much worse now than they were earlier.'

'I don't know why God is punishing us like this? What had we done bad to him? After praying for the past 20 years to him, I am getting this in return. How can he do this to us?' Mom began to sob.

'Don't cry, Mom. It has nothing to do with you. I must have done something in my past life which is making me suffer in this life.'

'Don't say this, beta. I can't see you like this for your whole life. God, please take my life and free my son from this curse. Free him from these nightmares.' Mom looked up, praying to God with folded hands.

'Stop it, Mom. Do you even think before saying such things?' I asked, but she kept mumbling something while looking upward for a few more seconds. 'Stop this, Mom. Whatever you are doing,' I shouted and stared at her with disgust.

'Fine. I am going to make tea for your father. If you also want, then tell me now only. I can't make it again and again on the individual demands of yours and your fathers.'

'Make one cup for me as well. I am going to our neighbors to see how the puppy is doing. I will be back in a few minutes.' Anjali opened the door on the first knock, which took me by surprise. This was the first time in my life anyone opened the door on the first knock. There I saw Anjali standing at the door wearing a t-shirt and shorts. The shorts were too short for her. Her thighs were completely visible in those shorts. I just stared at her long shiny legs with my open mouth, and she caught me looking at her.

'Are you coming inside or just want to stand here and stare at my legs?' She said while looking straight into my eyes and gave me a naughty smile. Her voice made me come out of the hypnosis, and I looked at her face.

'What? What you were saying?' I asked.

'Nothing. Come inside,' said Anjali and walked inside, leaving the door wide open. Looking at her, walking in those shorts, made me follow her. I came inside and locked the door behind me. I couldn't stop myself from staring at Anjali's back in those shorts. Just when I closed the door, the puppy came running toward me from the other room and began to lick my feet. I picked her up in my arms and caressed her. She cuddled in my arms and gave a little howl.

'I think she likes you. Look at her howling. She didn't howl even once after you left her here with me,' Anjali said and sat on the sofa. I walked to the couch holding the puppy and sat next to Anjali.

'Have you thought of a name for her yet?' Anjali questioned.

'No, I thought about it. But I can't pick a name for her on my own. I think it would be better if Kirti gives her a name as it is her birthday gift after all.' The puppy was trying to bite my finger with her tiny teeth.

'Yeah. I suppose you are right. Otherwise, she's again going to make a scene,' said Anjali. The puppy jumped from my lap onto the floor and ran off into the bedroom, howling.

'Did you order a cake for Kirti yet?'

'No. Not yet. I will call the Gupta's bakery tomorrow morning.'

'Okay. So, where is the birthday girl?'

'She went to some party at her friend's house. She didn't tell the name of her friend, but went out fully dressed.'

'Oh! Good for her. I am so happy for her. She is enjoying her life to the fullest. I mean, she married you, what more could she ask for.'

'I don't think so. I think she doesn't even love me anymore. If she did, then she would never behave the way she does these days,' I said in a fed-up tone. When I completed my sentence, Anjali laid down on the sofa and placed her head on my lap.

'What are you doing? What if someone sees us like this?'

'Don't be a kid. No one is home. No one will not see us,' Anjali said with excitement.

'What if Anuj comes and finds us like this? God knows what he will do then.'

'Oh, he won't be coming here anymore,' Anjali said with a wink.

'And why is that? He is your boyfriend. He can come any time he likes.'

'Not anymore. We broke up two weeks earlier. I told him I like someone else, we had a small fight, and we broke up.'

'Oh! So, who do you like? Who is that lucky guy?' I asked curiously.

'You are so dumb, Pranav. Of course, It's you. I don't sit with every guy with my head in their lap,' she said and rolled her eyes at me.

'Anjali, I am married to your friend. Even if I wanted to, I can't be with you. I have told you this before. Have you forgotten all that?'

'No, I have not. But it's okay if you don't love me back. I expect nothing in return from you, but just don't stop talking to me like you did earlier. I can't bear that. I can't live without you,' said Anjali, and tears rolled out from her eyes. Looking at her like this triggered something in me. *Your entire life, you were looking for a girl who would love you more than anything, and now that you have found her, you are rejecting her. What kind of person are you?* My inner self asked me. Listening to my inner voice, I slid the hair away from Anjali's face, bent down, and kissed her. In no time, the gentleness turned into craziness, and we began to kiss each other like animals. She put her tongue in my mouth and made me lick it.

'You are a nasty kisser,' I mumbled, but she pulled my face close to her and again kissed me.

'I want you inside me. I have been waiting for this moment for the last one month. I want you to make me feel the same way you did last time,' she said in an aroused tone.

'What do you mean by last time? What are you talking about?' That day too you said the same thing. That time I thought you were kidding with me, but now again, you said that.' I pushed her away from me.

'You mean, you don't remember? How can you forget about having sex with me? I sometimes feel you get mood swings too. One moment you are a different person and the next moment, your personality changes completely. I think something is wrong with you.' Her words made me feel as if millions of bees were stinging me at the same time. Suddenly, I felt a pain in my head. With every passing second, the pain increased and made me feel drowsy. I grabbed Anjali's neck and tried to choke her. I had no control over my body. She tried to shout, but my grip was too tight, which didn't let the words come out of her mouth. Her face went red and finally changed to blue. With every passing second, she was moving one step closer to death.

'What did you say? You think I get mood swings. You are damn right, and I will show you now, what these mood swings can make me do.' Out of nowhere, Anjali kicked me in my abdomen and got out of my grip.

'What the fuck is wrong with you, man? You nearly killed me. You are insane. I am calling the police right now.' Anjali panicked.

'I am so sorry, Anjali. I don't know why I did that. I don't know what got into me. Please don't call the police. I am really sorry. I don't know what happened to me,' I mumbled.

'Pranav, get the hell out of here. I don't want to see you anymore. Never show your face to me again, and take your fucking dog with you.' I went to the bedroom, picked up the puppy, and went out of her house before she killed me. I knocked on our flat's main door, but no one came to open it. I banged my fist on the door with intense force, and finally, my mother opened it.

'Where were you? Your tea is all cold. Why does your face look a little stunned to me? It looks like you just saw a ghost. Are you okay, beta?' Mom asked me while staring at my face.

'Nothing, I am okay,' I lied and went inside. As soon as I placed the puppy on the floor, she began to roam around the room. She went toward the pedigree bag, and after sniffing, she started whining.

'She must be hungry. That is why she is whining like this,' Mom said and went to get a bowl for her. She poured some pedigree in the bowl and placed it in a corner. When the puppy smelled the bowl filled with pedigree, she began to eat it like crazy. If an outsider looked at her eating, they would ask us, why not feed your dog from time to time?

'Has Kirti come back yet?' I asked, scratching my head.

'No. I tried to call her many times, but her number is unreachable,' Mom said while caressing the pup.

'But she told me she would be back by 6 p.m. and it is 8:30 p.m. She didn't even call to let me know she will be late.'

'Call her friends. They must know where she is. They can tell when she will be coming,' Mom said, still moving her hand over the puppy. Listening to her, I picked up my phone and called Kirti's friend Sunena Gupta. It rang two times and finally, she received the call.

'Hello. Who is this?' Sunena asked.

'Hey. It's Pranav on this side. Kirti's husband.'

'Hi, Pranav. How are you? How is your writing going on?' she asked curiously.

'I am good. My next novel will be released next month. My publishers are binding up everything and have started to plan the book promotions.'

'That is so great. Don't forget to send me a signed copy,' she said and giggled.

'Sure. I will parcel you the copy. Listen, I called you to ask about Kirti.'

'What about her? Why are you asking me about Kirti? She is your wife. You are supposed to know everything about her, not me,' she again giggled.

'Actually, Kirti has not come home yet. She went to some party, I just thought if you also were there too maybe you can tell me when will she be back? She told me she will be returning by 6 p.m.'

'Really? But she left the party around 5 p.m. She said she had some urgent work at home, and left early.'

'But there was no urgent work at home. Why would she say that?'

'I don't know that. She has never lied to me before.'

'Oh, okay. We are trying to call her, but her number is unreachable. This never happened earlier.'

'I will let you know if I get to know anything about her. If she reaches home, please then inform me.'

'Sure. I will do that. Thanks for the information. Bye,' I said and hung up. Then I called Kirti's other friends, but some told me they were not invited to any party, and some told Kirti left the party by 5 p.m. I even called my in-laws, but they didn't have any information about Kirti. I started to panic. 'Mom, I have called all of Kirti's friends, and they all told me that Kirti left the party by 5 p.m. She even lied by telling them that she had urgent work at home.'

'Really, she said that? Why would Kirti lie to them?' Mom asked in a puzzled voice.

'I don't know. Mom, I am getting worried now. What if something happened to her?'

'Don't say these things. Meri bahu ko kuch nahi ho sakta. Nothing can happen to my bahu. She will be back any minute now,' Mom said with surety.

'I don't know, Mom. I am getting this feeling as something has happened to her. I have no other option but to call the police,' I said in broken words.

'Are you mad, Pranav? Don't be a fool. She will come back. Believe me. There is no need to call the police at this time,' Mom said. But my mind failed to grasp the words she spoke. I picked up my phone and dialed the 1094 number, which was supposed to be called to report the missing person. After three long rings, someone finally picked the call.

'Hello. I am constable Sushant Verma speaking from Hennur Police Station. How may I help you?' a man said in a heavy voice.

'Hello Sir. My name is Pranav Sharma. I am calling to file a missing person's report. My Wife, Kirti Sharma went for a party at her friend's place, but she has not come home yet.'

'Calm down Sir. Sir, there is no need to panic. Bangalore police are there for your help. Now tell me when did Mrs. Kirti go to this party?' Constable Sushant Verma enquired.

'She left the house around 9 a.m. And she was supposed to come home by 6 p.m. She had a handbag with her, nothing else,' I answered.

'I am sorry Sir, but we can't file your complaint at this moment. We only have the authority to file a missing person's report after 24 hours. You will have to call us back tomorrow if your wife does not come back by then,' The constable said and hunk up on me.

'What happened? Whom are you calling at this hour?' Papa asked and sat next to me.

'Kirti has not come home yet. So, he is panicking. He thinks something has happened to her; that's why she hasn't come back,' Mom told my father in a calm tone as if nothing had happened.

'She will come back. Maybe she went to have a drink with her friends. You only said she has been drinking,' Papa said while picking up the television remote and finally switched it ON.

'Let's have dinner. She can eat whenever she comes. We are not going to wait for Maharani Kirti's arrival.' My mother taunted Kirti and went to the kitchen. We ate our dinner in complete silence. No one uttered a single word the entire time. After dinner, Mom collected all the dirty dishes and went to the kitchen to wash them. Papa sat there next to me watching the Discovery Channel. They both were behaving so normally as nothing was wrong. So, what if Kirti was missing? We can find a new bahu for us. They must be thinking, I thought. We watched the television for the next half hour.

'Go to sleep, beta. Get some rest. It is too late now. We don't know when will she be back, or if she is even coming back or not. Don't waste your sleep for her. Leave the main door open. She can come whenever she wants to.' Mom and papa both went to their room, leaving me on my own when I needed them the most. I turned off the television and rested on the sofa. Lying there, I thought about the incident with Anjali, thought about Kirti and Aarohi. All the women I have been within my life, I thought about them. Suddenly, I heard a gentle woof and felt something near my feet. When I looked, I saw the puppy lying on my legs. I picked her and placed her next to me on the sofa. She cuddled with my arms and fell asleep in no time. Looking at her sleeping helped me to calm myself. When no one is with me, then she is there with me to give me company. I will never forget this, I told myself.

'You are here with me when no one else is. You are my best friend. I will call you BUDDY from now on. Are you listening? Your name is BUDDY,' I whispered in her ears, but she just ignored my words and kept dozing with her eyes partially open. Looking at her sleeping also made me feel sleepy, and I yawned. I closed my eyes and prayed to God to help Kirti if she is in any trouble and went to sleep thinking about my lost wife.

*

'Wake up, Pranav beta. WAKE UP,' my mother shouted. Buddy started to bark when she heard my mom. Their voices stung in my head and made me uneasy. 'Kirti has not come back yet. Maybe you were right. Maybe something bad has happened with my bahu.' Mom started sobbing. As soon as I heard the word "Kirti", something triggered inside me. I woke up and stared at my mother with partially open eyes.

'What time is it?' I rubbed my eyes.

'It is 11:20 a.m. Beta, I am worried about Kirti now. We have still not informed Kirti's parents about her disappearance. Do you want me to call them?' Mom asked in a worrying tone.

'What will we tell her parents that their daughter went to a party and didn't come back?'

'I think so. That is the truth. What will we tell them otherwise? Do you have some other thing in mind?'

'Stop it Mom. I will call them later. Let me call the police first. We have to file the missing complaint.' I picked up the phone to call Hennur Police station. Someone received my call on the first call.

'Hello. This is ACP Arjun Singh speaking from Hennur Police station. How can I help you?' a man spoke on the other side of the call.

'Hello Sir. My name is Pranav Sharma. I called yesterday to file a report about a missing person. My wife, Kirti Aggarwal, has been missing since yesterday. She went to a party at her friends' place but didn't return home yet.'

'Pravu, is that you? Don't you recognize my voice? It's Arju,' said ACP Arjun Singh.

'Arju! Bete tu kab ACP ban Gaya. When did you become ACP?' I asked with amusement.

'It is a long story, brother. I will tell you later. Tu Bhabhi Ji Ke baare mein bata. Tell me what happened to Kirti? When did she leave home and what was she wearing at that time?' Arjun started the interrogation.

'She left around 9 a.m. for a party at her friend's place. She was wearing a magenta-colored saree at that time and had a brown handbag with her.' I answered Arjun's question with sincerity.

'Do you know the name of her friend whose home Kirti went to for the party?'

'I don't know the name of the friend. I didn't ask her that. I didn't know she was going to disappear just like that. If I had known, I would have asked her.'

'Bro, what I am going to ask you now is very important. Don't take it personally, but I have to ask these questions. It's the general procedure. Do you think Bhabhi is having an affair with another man?' Arjun asked in a low voice, trying not to offend me.

'Maybe, maybe not. I mean, I never noticed something like this with her. But a few days back, a man came to drop her home when she was drunk. But he wasn't that good-looking. So, I don't think he is worthy of having an affair with.'

'Okay. I have noted all the details and will call you if I need any more details from you. You might also have to come down to the station, so don't panic about it. I promise you, Pranav, I will find my Bhabhi.

We will do everything to find Kirti,' Arjun spoke with surety.

'Thank you, Bhai. I will wait for your call,' I said while trying to hold back my tears and hung up. Uncontrollable tears flowed from my eyes like water flows from a damaged tap.

'Why is this happening to us, Mom? First Aarohi and now Kirti. I think I am the cursed one, not my nightmares. Maybe it is my fate, whatever is happening to me. I am destined to lose everyone I love. I am the cursed one.' I started weeping like a child.

'Please don't cry beta. Everything will be alright. I have the gut feeling that the police will find Kirti in a few days. Give them some time. Time will make everything correct. Time is everything. Time is the cure for everything,' she spoke while caressing my back. Buddy was howling while sitting on the floor, as she too knows what I'm going through. After all, she is my BUDDY. She knows everything.

CHAPTER 17

The Letter

'I can't believe she is dead. If I had known she would die, I would have never let her go. I told her many times that bungee jumping is very dangerous, but she ignored me at that time. Now see what happened. I knew something bad would happen to her, and look; she is dead now. I said to my father and began to sob.' I typed on my laptop. I was trying to write this chapter for a few weeks now but was unable to complete it. I could not concentrate on my writing for the last few months. A lot of things were on my mind, and one of them is Kirti. It's been two years since Kirti left for the party and never came back. She just vanished in the air, and her whereabouts no one knows. I haven't received a message, a call, or a letter from her since she went somewhere. Police told us they did their best, whatever they could have done, but couldn't find any evidence that could solve the mystery of Kirti's disappearance. They finally closed her case. There has not been a single day when I had not called Kirti since the day she disappeared. But the only reply I ever got was, *'the number is unreachable.'*

There are two theories according to parents predicting what had happened to Kirti. My father thinks she ran away with her lover and settled in some foreign country. Most probably with the guy who came to drop drunk Kirti on that night at home. According to my mother, someone kidnapped Kirti and by mistake, killed her, and hid her body somewhere. But they are just stories for me, nothing else. Nobody knows what happened to Kirti in reality. Until I see the proof of her death, I won't believe in any of these stories. I am willing to wait for the rest of my life for Kirti, but I can't believe in them, and I won't. The past two years were tough for me. Anjali took Anuj back and shifted to his flat after our incident, I was broken into pieces. Some part of my heart still believes that Kirti will come back. I don't know when, but surely, she will come back someday. When my parents couldn't see me in pain anymore, they forced me to return to Delhi. They said a change in my surroundings will help me forget Kirti.

But as you can see this time too, it doesn't work at all similarly when my parents asked me to marry to cure my nightmare disorder in the first place. The Non-stop train of my thoughts was shattered when the doorbell rang. The loud sound of the bell stung in my ears and helped me to come back to reality. The reality in which I have lost my wife, my girlfriend, and Anjali's unrequited love for me.

'Beta, can you please open the door? I am busy making chapatis for breakfast,' Mom shouted from the kitchen.

'Mom, I am working right now. You go, please.' She knew the lazy me and finally went to check who was at the door. Suddenly, I heard my mother shouting. I stood up in a hurry and ran toward the door to check what happened. When I reached the main door, I saw my mother holding an envelope in her hands and staring at it.

'What happened, Mom? Why were you shouting? Is everything okay?' I asked in a worried tone.

'Beta, I think this letter is from Kirti,' Mom mumbled. The shock from hearing the word 'Kirti" generated a chill deep down my spine. My mind stopped thinking, and my body froze like ice.

'Sir, I don't have much time. Please sign here, and I will take leave,' The postman said, pointing to a piece of paper in his hand. His words helped me to regain my consciousness. He handed me a pen, and I signed on the paper and thanked him. As soon as I signed, he left in a hurry.

'Beta, who could have sent this letter? Kirti couldn't have sent it, as she is dead.'

'She is not dead, Mom. How many times do I have to tell you that?' I grabbed the envelope from her hand.

'Are you going to open it, or should I open it for you?' Mom said and looked at my black face.

'No. I will open it myself.' I went to my room and locked the door from inside. Mom knocked on the door a few times, but I didn't open it, even after many knocks. She finally stopped knocking. I sat on my bed and stared at the envelope for a few minutes. In bold letters was the name 'Kirti' written on it. I noticed it didn't have any return address on it. What can be in this? Who would have sent this? Even if Kirti has sent this, why now? Why, after two fucking years? I thought. A million questions sprouted in my mind, and to know their answers, I finally opened the envelope. I pulled out the piece of paper from the inside of the envelope and looked at it. I immediately recognized Kirti's handwriting. It was right from the beginning what I have been saying for the past two years. She is not dead. This letter is proof of her existence, I told myself. Controlling the erupting volcano of emotions inside me, I started reading the letter.

'Hello, Pranav. Firstly, I want to tell you that I am fine. If you thought I was dead, well I am not. Nothing had happened to me. Now, I know many questions are coming to your mind, and I promise you, I will be answering each of them when we meet personally. Why did I start behaving awkwardly when we moved to Bangalore? What forced me to start drinking? Why did I leave? Where did I go? I will answer all of them. It's pretty normal if you are surprised by this letter after all of these years. If I were at your place, then I would have felt the same. I want to meet you very urgently. I can't talk to you over the call, as the police must be tracking my phone number. So, I am writing this letter to you. Send me a letter at the address mentioned on the back of this paper

mentioning the location where we can meet. At last, I want to let you know I had your child. It is a baby girl. Our baby girl. I will tell you her name when we meet. Waiting for your letter. Bye.'

I was in shock when I finished reading the letter. When I got to know that leaving me was Kirti's own choice, I felt numb. She left me willingly. Why would she do something like that? Where did she go? Many questions sprouted in my mind, and she didn't give me even a single answer in the letter. I turned the paper around and saw an address written there where I was supposed to send her the letter.

'R-401, Ninth Floor, Connaught Place, New Delhi' I read the address and went into shock. It was the address of Kirti's parent's home. But why had she given me her parent's address? I scratched my head in puzzlement. Nothing came to mind, so I stopped brainstorming. Finally, I took a blank A4 paper from the printer, picked a blue ball pen, and wrote.

'Hello, Kirti. I feel a burden lifted from my shoulder knowing that you are alive. I am happy to know that you are okay. My parents told me their side of stories predicting what had happened to you, and their stories scared the shit out of me. Thank you for sending me the letter. Yes, I do want to know the answer to all the questions that you mentioned in your letter. I am dying to know why you left me. Following written is the address where we can meet. My publishers had arranged an author's interview for me next week at Mahatma Public library. We can meet there after the interview. I am asking you to meet me outside the house because I don't want to shock my parents with your sudden arrival. I am looking forward to meeting you. Bye. Take care. Love you.

The address is Mahatma Public library, Old Delhi Railway Station, Next to Chandni Chowk Metro Station Gate No. 1. Old Delhi- 110006.' I folded the paper carefully, placed it inside the envelope, and went to the nearby post office to post it.

'Sir, you want to post the letter in the same city? Is this some prank, or are you out of your mind?' said the worker sitting on the other side of the window. What he was saying is true, but I didn't have any other way to contact Kirti.

'No. It is not a prank. I want to post this letter very urgently. I am going to pay the whole shipping amount,' I mumbled and looked at the worker with stalking eyes.

'Fine. No problem, Sir.' He took the envelope from my hand. He glued a stamp on the envelope and asked for 50 rupees for the postal charge. I paid the required amount. While returning home I felt my heartbeat getting faster. I felt as if I am getting a heart attack. I stood on the roadside and took some long breaths. There I saw a small shop of Nimbu Pani and went there to have one drink. Just when I took one sip of it, my entire body cooled down. After finishing my Nimbu Pani, I went straight home to tell Mom about the letter.

CHAPTER 18

The Revelation

'Wake up, Pranav beta? Get up and have a bath. You will get late for the interview. Kirti is coming there to meet you. Did you forget?' Mom shouted from the kitchen. Her sharp tone of voice stung in my ears. I felt something moving in my blanket and coming toward me. I removed my blanket and saw Buddy crawling toward me. She came near my face and started licking it. She kept licking and finally howled as she wanted to wake me up. 'Wake up, Pranav. WAKE UP...' Mom shouted again.

'I am already up Mom. Please stop shouting.' I woke up and sat on the bed for a while. Buddy jumped in my lap and began to cuddle. I picked my Smartphone to check my messages. There were few, and I replied to them. It was already 10 a.m., and my interview was supposed to begin by noon. I stood up, picked a vest and briefs from my wardrobe, and went to take a bath. After the bath, I changed into the same Navy-blue suit I wore when I met Kirti for the first time. I wanted to begin a new journey with Kirti, so I thought of wearing the same suit.

'Mom, where is my breakfast? I don't want to be late for the interview,' I shouted.

'Coming beta. Waiting for two more minutes is not going to make you late.' She brought me some sandwiches and coffee. I started gulping my sandwiches without chewing them properly.

'Beta, Eat your breakfast properly. Don't be in such a hurry. Or do you want me to slap you and teach you a lesson on how to eat?'

'Mom, I am in a hurry. You know that.' I took the last bite and gulped it in half-chewed.

'Is Kirti coming back with you home after the interview?' Mom asked.

'I don't know, Mom. I don't even know if she is coming to meet me or not.' I finished my coffee, and I stood up to leave when Mom called me from behind. I turned around and saw a bowl in her hand.

'Beta has some Dahi. It's for good luck,' Mom requested.

'Fine, Mom.' I walked to her, and she fed me two spoons of sweetened curd, and I touched her feet before leaving, and I went out. When I came out of the lift, I saw the ola taxi parked outside our building, which I booked a few minutes earlier. I told him my name, and he confirmed my ride. I entered the cab, and he began to drive. He dropped me in front of the Mahatma Public library in forty minutes. Finally, I paid him the fare, and he left. I didn't expect Mahatma Public library to be such a luxurious work of art, but the building's structure and design blew my mind away. The library was painted in red with a shade of gold at distinct parts. I stood there for a few seconds to admire the beauty of the building. The train of my thoughts stopped when I heard someone calling my name.

'Hey Pranav. Here, look to your left.' It was Mr. Shubham Sinha from Metro Publishers who called my name and waved at me to get my attention. It took me a few seconds to figure out the source of the voice. I saw Shubham waving at me and I walked toward him.

'Why standing there? You are already fifteen minutes late?'

'Sorry, Shubham. I woke up late,' I said, and we started walking. We entered the library, and everyone stood up from their seats and clapped for us. I was overwhelmed by the gesture, and I sat on the chair which had my name on it with pride. I realized that the person who was supposed to take my interview was late too. A few minutes later, I saw a man entering the hall and walked toward me.

'Hello Sir. I am Keshav Kashyap. I am supposed to be conducting your interview today. I am extremely sorry to keep you waiting. There was some emergency at my home, hence the delay.' He made an apologetic face.

'Hi, Keshav. There is no need to feel sorry. I came in late too. We can start whenever you are ready.'

'Sure Sir. We will be starting the interview as soon as our special guests come. How can we start without them? After all, they are sponsoring the event,' Keshav said with a twinkle in his eyes.

'Who is coming? No one told me that there will be any special guests in the event too,' I asked in confusion.

'Yes, Sir. It is a surprise for you. They will be here any minute now.' He looked at the main door. A few minutes later, the special guests arrived. When they stepped into the hall, everyone stood up to greet the sponsors of today's event. All of the people in the room were clapping except me. I was shocked to see who the special guests were. My mind was not able to grasp anything. I froze in my seat and kept staring at them. Mr. Kapil Aggarwal, Mrs. Madhuri Aggarwal, and Kirti holding a baby, walked toward the stage and sat on their respective chains. A couple in their 50s also walked in and sat next to the Aggarwal family. I was still in shock when Mr. Keshav started speaking.

'Good afternoon everyone. Today with us is the best-selling author of 15 fiction books, Mr. Pranav Sharma. Accompanying him is his wife, Kirti Sharma, and his in-laws. We have two special guests with us too, but we will introduce them in a few minutes. Without wasting any time, let us begin the author's interview.' Mr. Keshav started the interview and asked me questions relating to my book and my personal life. The interviewing session went on for more than an hour, and afterwards, it was time for the crowd to ask questions to me. After twenty minutes, Mr. Keshav Kashyap ended the event. Just when people were getting up to leave the hall, Kirti stood up from her chair and started speaking.

'Hello everyone. I am just going to take a few more minutes of your time. Please sit back at your respective seats.' She took out a diary from her bag.

'What the fuck is this, Kirti? What diary is that?' I shouted with no control over me. But Kirti just ignored my words and kept speaking.

'Today, I am here to show you all the real face of Mr. Pranav Sharma. I know you might not be able to believe what I say, but it is the bitter truth.' I could see tears rolling down from Kirti's eyes. 'This diary was written by Aarohi Aggarwal, whom my husband murdered,' Kirti cried out loud and showed the diary to the crowd.

'Shut the fuck up, you bitch. I will kill you,' I shouted with no control of myself and suddenly stood up to get the diary from Kirti. The crowd started murmuring. Just then, three men wearing police uniforms entered the hall and walked toward the stage. I ran toward Kirti and snatched the diary from her hands. But I was too late. A policeman took the diary from my hand and gave it to Kirti, and placed a handcuff on my hands.

'What the fuck are you doing? Do you know who I am? I am going to kill you all,' I began to shout uncontrollably and tried to free my arms from their grip.

'Take this bastard from here. He is a murderer. He killed Aarohi, my cousin. He killed their daughter.' Kirti pointed at the couple who came with her and spit on my face. One of the constables held my shirt's collar and dragged me out of the library. They made me sit in their jeep and finally drove to the Delhi police station.

'Calm down, beta. Everything is okay now. They took him with them to the police station. We did it. Our plan was successful.' Mrs. Aggarwal tried to calm Kirti down. She helped Kirti to sit on the chair and gave her some water.

'What is in this diary, Kirti? What is it all about?' Mr. Keshav asked Kirti with curiosity.

'This is a diary written by Aarohi, Pranav's ex-girlfriend. If you all want to know what's in it, I can read it for you all. The real truth of Mr. Pranav Sharma is written in it,' Kirti said while sobbing.

A man from the crowd shouted, 'Read it.' Joining him, others also began to scream. At last, everyone in the hall sang in unison, 'Read it. Read it. Read it.' Listening to the crowd, Kirti began to read Aarohi's diary to the crowd from the beginning.

AAROHI'S DIARY

Monday, August 29, 2016

'Hi' or 'Dear Diary'? What should I start with? I have never written in a diary before, but still, I am writing one. I am starting a new chapter in my life and I want to remember it. Not for my kids or my family. I am writing it for myself. I want to note down every moment of my life from today onwards.

Let me introduce myself. I am Aarohi Aggarwal. One and only daughter of Mr. Avtar and Mrs. Sunita Aggarwal. After a lot of hard work and scoring good marks, I finally got admission to the University of Delhi. I will be studying Computer science and Engineering there. My college will be starting from 1st September, and I am terrified of leaving home. The thing is, I have never stayed out of my home. Not even for a week, and here we are talking about completing four years of living all alone at a hostel. Even thinking about it is making me sweat. I have no idea what kind of people I will meet there. But what I know for sure is that I will make many friends from the first day itself. It's my gift. I am an extrovert by nature. I can talk for hours, but only if the other person is taking an interest in the conversation. I hope everything goes perfectly, and these four years go by in the blink of an eye.

Mom is shouting from her room asking me to sleep. I have an early train tomorrow at 7 a.m. and I am traveling alone to Delhi. I just wanted to start writing my first ever journal before I went to sleep. Let's see how it goes. I am going to sleep now, otherwise, I might end up missing my train. I hope everything goes well. Fingers crossed. See you tomorrow, dear diary. Bye.

Tuesday, August 30, 2016

I woke up at around 5:30 a.m. Mumma had packed my bags, and I didn't have the slightest idea of what stuff was packed in there. Mumma and Papa came to the station to drop me. I wept like a kid when the train started. Looking at me crying, tears rolled out from my parent's eyes, and we hugged. Before leaving, Mumma said to me, 'Beta, you will meet different people in college. Remember, the type of person you will become depends on what kind of people you spend time with. Please don't embarrass us by doing something stupid. Our family's respect is now in your hands.' I didn't fully understand what she wanted to say, but I got the gist of it.

All the seats in the trains are fully packed, it is a bit suffocating. I had booked a lower seat, which is better for me as I can't climb up and down again and again for the upper berth. Most people aren't wearing their socks, and the odor from their feet is making it very difficult for me to breathe. Today is the third day of my periods, and I feel like doing nothing. For the whole day, I just lay on my seat and read 'Norwegian Wood' by Haruki Murakami. Murakami's writing is just outstanding. When I read his books, I feel alive and out of the world. I don't know him personally, but he is helping me pass my time through the journey. Our train is still 300 kilometers away from Delhi. The estimated time to reach H-Nizamuddin station is around 8 a.m. I hope the train is on schedule and reaches Delhi on time.

It is 11 p.m., I am going to sleep now. I had been reading non-stop for the past three hours, and now my eyes are hurting. Tomorrow, I have to wake up early, so it's time to sleep. See you soon, dear diary. Bye.

Thursday, September 1, 2016

I don't feel like writing today, but still, I am writing for just the sake of adding an entry in my diary. The train journey made me very tired today. All the joints in my body are hurting and making my life like hell. I didn't know what the builders thought when they built the girl's hostel college building, too far from the college. They must be high on something, I suppose.

On top of that, my periods are still on. I know being a girl, I have to go through this phase every week a month, but sometimes I think, why us? Why only women? Why not men? I even asked my Mumma about this, to which she said, 'Men are not that strong. They only pretend to be tough, but they are not. That's why God only made us women in this way and gifted us the capability to be mothers.' At that time, I believed whatever she said but now when I remember her saying, I think she just wanted to make me feel good, so she lied to me.

I got a room in Girls Hostel 1, and my roommate's name is Charu Gupta. Let me tell you something about Charu. I saw her for the first time when I entered the room allotted to us. When I looked at her, I sensed something was going on with her. I didn't know what, but something fell off about her. Charu locked her eyes with mine when I stepped into our room, and from then on, she was behaving awkwardly around me. I started talking to Charu, and she told me that she is from Rohtak, Haryana, and studied at a Girl's school from the beginning. At first, she hesitated to open up, but later, she felt comfortable and shared all of her secrets with me.

I also met another girl, Gita Mishra. I met her for the first time in the office where hostel rooms were being allocated to the newly admitted students. She was standing in front of me in the line, and suddenly she turned toward me and asked my name. I told her my name, and just like that, we talked the whole time. I liked having a conversation with her, and I think she also felt the same. She must have, as later she asked me if I wanted to share the room with her, and I agreed with her. But when we told the warden we wanted to share a room, she told us it is not possible. Room allotment is done strictly according to the alphabetic order, and there is no way we will get the same room. Gita becomes sad after hearing the warden. We both were sad at that moment as we wanted to be roommates.

Later, when I was arranging my stuff in my room, Gita came running to my room. She was all out of breath and sweating. I asked her what happened. Why is she running like that? In reply, she said she got a room on the same floor as mine. She just wanted to give me this news.

Gita, Charu, and I went to college together. How great it would have been if everyone turned toward me and admired my beauty. I wanted this to happen, but obviously, that didn't happen. No one turned around, and no one admired my beauty. We sat in the second row from the front. Later, a professor came to our room to take our first lecture. He introduced himself to us. His name was Mohan Shrivastava, and he will be teaching us the Basics of programming. After the class had begun, a guy entered the lecture hall and took a seat next to Gita. When the lecture got over, he started talking with Gita. He said his name is Jatin Verma.

At last, he asked for Gita's contact number. I don't know why, but Gita also exchanged her number with him. When he left, I wondered why Gita gave him her number. I told her she shouldn't have given her number to a guy she just met. But she said he was too cute. And she was not wrong, he was adorable.

We came to our hostel after our classes. Gita came to our room around 5 o'clock, and we revised all the subjects and then went to have dinner. Hostel food tastes nothing like food cooked by mothers' hands, but it will do. It will keep us alive for the next 4 years, and that's what matters. This is all that happened today. Now my head is going to burst if I don't stop writing and go to sleep. See you, dear diary. Bye.

Monday, September 5, 2016

Things are going serious between Gita and Jatin pretty fast. Charu and I can't figure out what happened to them so suddenly. We have officially announced them as Love birds. For the past few days, Jatin has been sitting with Gita in the lecture hall and hanging out with us after college. Gita is going mad about Jatin, I think. It's been only a few days since they met and already began to behave so weirdly. They spend all their time together. It's not like I am jealous of Gita. I am more than happy for her, and my best wishes are always with them. But she has to find the balance between her love life and academics. They sit together in the lecture hall and keep whispering to each other during lectures. I want to tell Gita to concentrate on her studies, but I don't want her to feel as if I am jealous of her. I really don't want to jeopardize our relationship.

My studies are going great. I like all of our teachers except some. Not because they don't know how to teach, but the real reason is they are rude. They don't know how to talk with their students. Like Yesterday, I forgot to keep my phone in silent mode, and in the middle of the lecture, it started ringing. Our professor gave me a look, and I enabled the silent mode. But to my bad luck, it rang again. I don't know how it's possible, but still, it happened.

Professor Suresh asked me to leave the classroom. I told him I was sorry. I tried to explain to him that I turned on the silent mode and didn't know how it rang again. But he was so stubborn and made me leave the class. 'I don't want any nonsense like this in my class. If you guys do not want to study, then there is no need to attend my lectures. This is not a zoo. It is a lecture hall, so you all learn how to behave in front of your professors.' Professor Suresh said to the class after I left, which Gita told me later. I felt horrible after hearing her, as there was no mistake from my side in what happened earlier. It took me some minutes to forget what happened in the classroom, and finally, I felt normal when my friends cheered me up.

Jatin came with us to drop Gita at our hostel as if she can't walk on her own. Love is blind, and it is definitely making them blinder day by day. Jatin said goodbye to Gita and he left. When we entered our room, Gita told me that some guy wanted to say something to me and that he will be meeting me tomorrow in the lecture hall. I asked her who he was, but she didn't know. I am lying in my cozy bed and still thinking about who it can be. Why does some guy want to meet a girl like me? I am a little nervous but excited too to meet the guy tomorrow. I will try my best to get some sleep before that. Bye.

Tuesday, September 6, 2016

Today, I woke up precisely at 6 a.m. But I haven't done it intentionally. Maybe because subconsciously, I was excited for today that my mind automatically settled a mental alarm and helped me wake up so early. Whatever it was, I am glad it happened. After scrolling through Instagram for a few minutes, I finally went to take a bath. Fifteen minutes later, I came back and saw Charu half-awake using her phone. When I entered the room, she gave a naughty smile to me and pulled my leg by saying, 'Oh hoo…Aaj Pati Dev ko Milne ki Khushi main ladki itni jaldi uth Gayi.' In reply, no words came to my mind, and I just blushed standing there. Hearing her, my cheeks turned into red Kashmiri apples. I kicked Charu, who was still lying on the bed, and ordered her to get a bath. Obeying my order like a good girl, she went to take a bath, still partially awake, faltering a little. I wanted to look good today. Not to impress someone, but I just felt like it.

Okay. Okay. Fine. I will not be lying to my dear diary ever. Yes, I want to impress the unknown guy, if really someone is coming to meet me. I wore my new purple top and blue jeans that Mom gifted me. Today is the best day to wear them, I thought. When Charu returned after bathing, she gave me a mischievous smile after seeing me all dressed up. 'Aaj to Dil jeetne ka irada hai ladki ka. Itna kahar mat dhao ji kahin humko hee na aapse pyar ho jaye.' Charu smiled ear to ear. Ignoring her, I finished dressing up and also forced her to do the same. A few minutes later, Gita came to our room, and we went to have breakfast.

We sat on our usual seats in the lecture hall. Three lectures got over, but there was no trace of Jatin anywhere in the room. I thought it was just a prank pulled on me by Jatin when he told me that someone was coming to meet me. I felt awful and wanted to cry. Professor Suresh came to take his lecture and began teaching as soon as he arrived in the room. I checked my phone and turned it off this time. I didn't want him to get mad at me again at any cost.

We were looking at the whiteboard with our total concentration when someone knocked on the door. Professor Suresh gestured to a guy sitting close to the door to check who was on the door. When he opened the door, Jatin entered the room with a blank face. A boy walked after him and stood next to Jatin. Looking at them arriving late for the class, Suresh gave them a quick speech and finally ordered them to sit. Jatin came to our bench and sat next to Gita, and the unknown guy took the seat next to Jatin. Looking at Jatin sitting next to Gita, Professor Suresh gave them a weird look and started to teach. I tilted back a little to look at the guy who came with Jatin but was only able to see a side view of his face. He had a little beard with a faded side hairstyle. He was cuter than I expected. Gita and Jatin again talked for the whole lecture as expected while holding hands. As soon as the lecture got over, Jatin introduced us to the guy. He told us that his name is Pranav Sharma, and he is a Civil Engineering student. After greeting the others, he came close to me to shake my hand. When he took my hand in his hand, I went blank. The intensity of my heartbeat increased when he touched me, and I said 'Hello' in a low tone and blushed.

We walked back to the hostel for lunch, and they both came with us. Jatin walked next to Gita and Pranav next to me. They all were having a good time and left me alone with the unknown guy. Then finally, he spoke while breaking the ice. 'Yesterday I asked Jatin to pass a message to you that I want to talk with you. Jatin told me about the incident that yesterday happened to you in the classroom. I don't know why, but after hearing him, I felt something and asked for your Instagram ID from Jatin. When I looked at your posts, I fell in love with you instantly. I read all of your poetry and quotes, which you uploaded on your account, and they amazed me. I know whatever I am saying is not making any sense to you, but I am only telling what I feel.'

'Oh, okay. I love to write in my leisure time. Thank you for saying such lovely words about my writing.'

'Don't take me in the wrong way, but I like you the moment I saw your picture. I loved your long hair and big eyes.'

'Thank you.' I said and blushed. Again, my cheeks turned into red Kashmiri apples, and Pranav just kept staring into my eyes. Finally, we reached our hostel. Before leaving, Jatin asked us if we wanted to go out for lunch tomorrow. Everyone instantly agreed to the plan. When they were leaving, Pranav turned around and smiled at me. In reply, I also gave an ear-to-ear smile and walked inside the hostel in a hurry. Looking at me like this, Charu and Gita started to pull my leg. Their words did not affect me, I was still hypnotized by the touch of Pranav's hand and just stared at my hand until we reached our hostel mess.

Wednesday, September 7, 2016

Dear diary, I had a dream about Pranav last night. It's not like I was thinking about him all the time since we came back from college. I mean, I was, but not all the time. In the dream, it was my birthday, and we went to a hotel to celebrate it. There I cut the cake which Pranav brought for me. While cutting the cake, he began to sing an old Hindi song by Kishore Kumar instead of singing the usual happy birthday song. 'Hamein tumse pyar kitna ye hum nahi jaante, Magar jee nahin sakte tumhare bina, Hamein tumse pyar kitna ye hum nahi jaante, Magar jee nahin sakte tumhare bina, Hamein tumse pyar kitna…' he sang and knelt down to propose me with a red rose in his hand. No words came out of my mouth, and I just stared at him. And finally, I said 'YES', and we kissed. Later, we made crazy love and slept in each other's arms.

My dream broke when my mental alarm rang and forced me to wake up without my consent. I checked my smartphone for any messages, scrolled through Instagram, and finally went to take a bath. When I came back from the bath, Charu was partially awake and listening to the 'Tum hi ho' song by Arijit Singh on the loudspeaker. Looking at her still partially sleeping, I went close to her bed and tried to kick her as usual. But this time, she grabbed my leg and pulled me close to her. The force she used to drag me was so strong that I banged my back on top of her bed. Looking at me in pain, she moved her head close to mine and kissed me on my lips.

'What the fuck, Charu? Are you mad or what?' I shouted and pushed her away from me, still rubbing my back. In reply, she didn't say anything and, in a hurry, went to take a bath. I don't know if she did that on purpose or not, but whatever the reason can be, I just didn't like it.

When Charu came back from the bath, she apologized to me. 'I don't know why I did that. I am so sorry. It will not happen again, I promise. Please don't mention this to anyone,' She uttered while concealing her eyes from mine and began to dress up. Finally, we went to have breakfast and met Gita there. After breakfast, we grabbed our backpacks and went to college.

Today, Jatin and Pranav arrived even earlier than us for the lecture. When we entered the lecture hall, they were sitting in our usual seats. I don't know why, but Gita made me sit next to Pranav. Pranav was sitting on my left side and Charu on my right. I didn't know what to talk about with Pranav. So, I just kept quiet, saving myself from saying something silly. Later, Pranav started talking about books, which is my favorite subject. My eyes lit up hearing him, and just like that, we talked for the whole lecture. He told me that writing is his passion. He is currently writing a novel, and he would love to have my opinion on it. I ask him why he does not attend his lectures? What will he do if his attendance does not cross the mark as required? In reply, he said he is a friend of his class representative, and he will take care of his attendance.

At lunchtime, we went to a small shop next to our college for lunch. Pranav asked me what I will have, and in response, I said I would have the same whatever he will have. A few minutes later, he came back with two plates of Samosas. We were having the usual conversation when suddenly Pranav asked for my WhatsApp number. It was so sudden that I choked on the bite of samosa. He helped me drink some water, and the water made me a little better. We exchanged our contacts at last. Charu, Gita, and Jatin finished their Dosa, and finally, we went back to the college.

When our college got over, Pranav and Jatin came with us back to our hostel to drop us off. Pranav was walking next to me, and our hands met. Out of nowhere, he held my hand in his and behaved as if nothing happened. I also didn't stop him, and we walked to the hostel holding hands like some couple madly in love. Before leaving, Pranav hugged me and whispered in my ears, 'Will wait to hold your hand again,' and they left.

I am currently lying in my bed and still feeling his touch. I think I am falling for Pranav. I know it is too fast, but it is what I am feeling. I am feeling something-something for him. I can't share my feelings with anyone at this moment, so I am sharing with only you, My Dear diary. Now, I am feeling tired and going to sleep. So, see you tomorrow. Bye.

Sunday, September 11, 2016

Dear diary, sorry for not adding an entry for some days. These days I have been spending a lot of time with Pranav. I really enjoy spending time with him. It's like he has put some spell on me, and the result is the more I think about him, the more I crave for him. I am falling more in love with him with each passing day. We talk on the phone all night. Few times, Charu even cursed me while sleeping and shouted to stop whispering over the phone late at night. After college, we go for long walks. We don't go to some fancy place. Instead, we just roam around on our campus while holding each other's hands. The thing is, I can't say no to him for anything. I don't know why I can't, but it is how it is. Whenever he asks me out for lunch or a movie, I immediately agree. The only words that come out of my mouth at these moments are, 'Fine. Let's go.'

Today also, he asked me to go out for dinner. We went to the famous Café Resto at Jaypee Vasant. He ordered two meals of Noodles and Manchurian for both of us. For the entire dinner, we talked while staring into each other's eyes, like we lost something inside one another. After dinner, he came back to drop me off at my hostel. I told him many times that I can go on my own, but he insisted and came with me. When we were returning to my hostel, the road was deserted. While walking out of nowhere, Pranav grabbed my waist and pulled me close to him. We were so close that I even felt his warm breath. In no time, my heartbeat increased, and I lost control over my body. I am sure he must have felt that as then he suddenly kissed me. I tried to stop him initially, but later I opened myself to him. We kissed each other hard and long, and then he began to caress my bosom. His gentle touch aroused me to the point where I started feeling wet down there. He tried to put his hand inside my panties, but I stopped him. I do like him, but I don't want to confuse our physical attraction with love. It's not like I didn't want him to please me, but we are not at that point yet. I told him I think that we are taking things too fast. Kissing is acceptable, but more than that, I can't do it. I want to, but I can't. I hope he understood what I wanted to say and didn't take it the wrong way. Finally, we reached my hostel. He gave me a good night's hug and left.

Now I am lying in my bed, thinking about him. What he did to me on that road, I can still feel him in every inch of my body. The way he grabbed my waist, pulled me close to him, and gently kissed me on my lips. Everything I am still feeling. I don't know if stopping him was the right decision or not, but I did what I felt right at that moment. I have to go to college tomorrow, so I am going to sleep. Today was a fabulous day of my life, and I wanted to preserve my feeling, so I told you as you are my best friend these days. Bye. See you soon.

Saturday, September 17, 2016

For the last few days, Charu has not talked to me. She even goes to the mess alone. I don't remember doing anything that would make her behave like this, but I couldn't see her like this anymore. So, I decided to confront. I wanted to know why she was behaving so weirdly for some days.

I was resting in my room when Charu came in. She placed her backpack on the bed and turned around to exit the room. Just then, I asked her where she was going?

'I don't think there is any need for us to talk. Friends do the talking, and we are no more friends.'

'What are you talking about, Charu? Did anyone say something to you? Please let me know if I had done anything to hurt you unintentionally?'

'If you want to listen, then listen. I thought we were friends, but I was wrong. I am nothing more than a thing of time passing for you. Now you are in a relationship, so I thought you don't need me anymore. You spend all the time with your psycho boyfriend, Pranav. But now I think you deserve only that scum.'

'Don't say these things about him. Yes, I love him, and if you have any problem with it, then get lost. I don't want a bitch like you as my friend,' I shouted with rage.

'You know I loved you. That day when I kissed you, I thought you also had feelings for me. But I know that fucker Pranav spoiled everything whatever we had between us. I still love you, Aarohi. Leave him for me, please. I will do all the things that he is doing for you. I mean everything. Are you getting what I am talking about?'

'Get out of the room, you bitch. I am not a lesbian like you. Now I know why you were behaving weirdly the day when we first met. I will tell everything to the warder lady if you do not get out of here right now,' I shouted. Hearing me, tears rolled from Charu's eyes, and she left the room in a hurry, still sobbing. I don't know whether what I said to her is fair to say or not, but I can't do what she asked me to do. I mean, I am not attracted to her. I am not a lesbian if she thinks. I don't want to talk to her anymore. I am thinking of shifting to some other room. I can't live with her anymore after what happened today. I am going to sleep before Charu comes back. I don't want to face her. Good night, dear diary. Bye.

Sunday, September 25, 2016

It's been some days when Pranav and I were sitting in the classroom when I told him about the incident with Charu. When I finished talking, he began to laugh with his mouth wide open. Looking at him, laughing at my screwed-up life, I punched him in his tummy, then only he stopped.

'Tell me yaar what do I do? I was thinking of changing my room?' I asked him and made a puppy face.

'You can do whatever you think is best for you. But if you ask me, I want to see you and Charu in some action,' Pranav said and continued laughing.

'Shut up. As you said this, now see, I will change my room for sure. No action you are getting, Mr. Pranav.' I taunted him. After college, I went to the hostel office and asked the warden lady if there is an empty room available in the hostel. She told me there is one, but it is only for a single person. I will take it, I said, and finally, I shifted there. Charu tried many times to change my mind and even apologized to me. But my mind was made, and I just ignored whatever she said.

Today, Pranav and I went to Central Park, Connaught Place. He told me he had planned a surprise for me there. So, I went there with him. We were sitting in the park and having a normal conversation when, out of nowhere, he keeled and asked me to be his girlfriend. Looking at him proposing to me, I became emotional and tired rolled down my eyes. He stood up and tried to calm me, which helped, and finally, I accepted his proposal.

Pranav was lying with his head in my lap and I asked him what would he do if my parents did not let him marry me? 'In that case, I will kidnap you from your home and take you with me somewhere where no one can find us. Then we will start our family, and we will live there happily for the rest of our life,' he said in response, which I felt was a bit childish thing to say. Listening to him, I told him I love him more than anything, but I can't leave my parents for him. I can't do such a cruel thing to my parents, as I know it will break them. He just kept quiet and made a blank face. Looking at him like this, I bent a little and kissed him. We made out for a bit, but then I made him stop. I am not comfortable being physical in such an open space, I told him. He understood and finally stopped. Then, I told him I am feeling tired from sitting for such a long time in the park and want to eat something. He took me to a mall, and we had momos there. Later, he brought me a fancy handbag which I didn't accept at first, but he forced me to keep it. We roamed in the mall for a few more minutes, and after spending quality time, he dropped me at my hostel and returned to his flat.

Thursday, September 29, 2016

Everything was going just perfectly until today. Pranav and I were going out for movies, shopping, for long walks, and whatnot. Earlier, I thought I am lucky and got the best boyfriend in the world. He doesn't drink like boys of his age. He is loyal and also cares so much about me. But there has to be something to spoil things up. Yes, he is not perfect. He has an anger management problem and some other issues, which I m still getting to know about.

Today, Professor Suresh was teaching us about functions topic in the C programming language when I felt a kick on my shoes from behind. I bent down a little to see what was going on and saw someone kicking me with their shoes from behind. I turned back to get a look at the person and saw a boy. When I looked at him, he began to kick my shoes non-stop and gave me a weird smile. He stopped for a few seconds and again resumed with his kicking. I couldn't take it anymore and told Pranav about it. Listening to me, Pranav didn't react for a few seconds, but out of nowhere, I don't know what happened to him. He began to shout while cursing. He stood up from his seat in a hurry and grabbed the shirt collar of the guy sitting behind us. I told Pranav to let him go, but he just ignored my words. The face of the guy turned blood-red in no time. Jatin also tried to stop Pranav, but Pranav kept pushing Jatin away from him.

Out of nowhere, Pranav punched the guy with his fist and kept hitting until blood flowed from his nostrils. When the situation went out of hand, Professor Suresh took charge and shouted, 'Stop it, guys. Enough is enough.' in a high-pitched voice. Listening to Professor Suresh's voice, pin-drop silence went all across the room, and everyone froze still at the position where they were. Pranav was breathing with high intensity when professor Suresh walked to him and slapped his face in full swing. The slap was of such force that the professor's hand's print was printed on Pranav's face. Then, out of nowhere, Pranav kicked professor Suresh in the stomach with his leg and went out of the classroom sprinting.

Looking at Pranav leaving, I went after him. He walked out of the university building and stopped in the middle of the road next to our department's entry. I walked to him. He was still looking a little psyche and was taking long breaths.

'Are you okay, Pranav? What happened to you in the classroom?' I asked him, but his focus was on his hand, and he just ignored my words. Later, he showed me his hand, which had a significant cut from the fight, and blood was flowing from it.

'What happened to your hand?' I asked him in a worrying tone.

'I don't know, baby. Why are we standing here? I can't remember anything.'

'What? What are you saying?' I asked in amazement, but he kept quiet. His hand's injury looked severe to me, so forcing him, I took him to a nearby hospital with me. We went to Primus Super Specialty

Hospital, where we met surgeon Ashish Choudhary. He asked us to do an X-ray of Pranav's hand. After getting done with the X-ray, we showed it to doctor Ashish. Analyzing the X-ray for a few seconds, he told Pranav's hand is fractured, and it needs to get plastered. After getting his hand plastered, I paid for the charges and exited from there. When we were walking out of the hospital, I heard someone calling Pranav while saying 'Pranav…Pranav beta…' in a sharp voice. We tried to figure out the source of the voice but failed. Just then, a doctor walked to us and asked about Pranav's health.

'Do you still have mood swings? Pranav beta, are you taking your medicine at the time?' the doctor asked. In reply, Pranav didn't say anything and just looked at the doctor's face. He had worn a white doctor's coat, and Dr. Ajay Thakur was written on his badge.

'I don't know you, sir. I can't remember who you are,' Pranav said and, while holding my arm, dragged me out of there. While returning I asked him if he still can't remember anything about what happened at college and in reply, he again said, 'No, I can't.' Later, I dropped him off at his flat and came back to my hostel.

It was all so strange. I still can't figure out how Pranav didn't remember the scene that happened in the lecture hall. I mean, I can't forget about it till my last breath, and he forgot about it just a few minutes after it happened. I think something is wrong with him. I was also thinking about what the doctor said about Pranav's mood swings. It is true. He does get mood swings quite frequently, but he doesn't know about them. I hope his health improves and whatever is going on with him stops. Today was a heck of a day. I am so tired. So, good night.

Wednesday, October 5, 2016

I don't feel like writing today. My mood is off, but I am still writing. My cousin Kirti called me today and gave me another thing to stress about. Like there is not enough drama going on in my life already. First Charu and now her. Kirti is the only daughter of my Papa's brother Kapil Aggarwal. We were very close to each other in our childhood. We used to do everything together. When we couldn't find each other, we used to cry our guts out. But as you know, when people grow, they change, and so did we. From our early childhood, her parents used to say, 'Look at Aarohi. She is so pretty. Why didn't God give our daughter a complexion like her? Why? How are we going to find a groom for her with this complexion?' Listening to them always taunting about her dark complexion, Kirti's love for me changed to hatred. Once, Kirti told me, 'You are making my life like living hell. Why do you have to be so pretty? Please let me live my life in peace from now on. You already have done enough. Now please leave me alone.' She never spoke to me since that day, and then she went to Bangalore for her higher studies. I never saw her again.

But I don't know why, after all these years, she called today. Pranav and I were having our lunch during the lunch break at the College's canteen when my phone rang.

'Hello, Aarohi. Your cousin Kirti this side. Hope I didn't disturb you.'

'No. I was free. I am delighted that you finally called after all these years. How is everyone at home? How is Chachu Ji doing?'

'Everyone is doing great. Papa is also fine. He is still at his office. You tell me how your life is going? I got to know you are studying Computer Engineering at the University of Delhi. Are you really?'

'Yes, I am. Everything is going great. Who told you about it? Mumma or Papa?'

'That's not important. Let's forget about it. So, have you made any boyfriend at college? Delhi's boys are really something. Don't you think?'

'I think so. Yes, I am in a relationship with a guy from our college. Please don't say anything about it to my parents. They will kill me if they get to know about it.'

'Don't you worry about that? Do you think I just let you go with such ease after what you made me go through in my childhood? I got enough information for which I called. Now see what I will do,' Kirti said and hung up on me.

I don't know what I thought when I told her about Pranav. I thought she must have forgotten about the things that happened in our childhood, but as you can see, she hasn't for sure. Kirti was looking for a perfect opportunity to take her revenge on me, and today I gave her the best chance to ruin my life served on a plate. If she tells anything about Pranav to my parents, then I am done. I still remember what my mother told me when we were at the station. It was not just a suggestion, instead, it was more like a warning. They will call me back home if they get to know about him. What if they get me married to some other guy? They can do anything for their pride. It's 8 o'clock right now, and I haven't yet received any call from my parents. For the past two hours, I have been sitting on my bed and staring at my phone, waiting for their call. I hope Kirti didn't tell my parents about Pranav, but the probability of this happening is relatively low. Let's see what happens. If I am brave enough to love someone, then I have to be ready to face its consequences too. Gita is at the door, knocking, again and again. It's dinner time. Now I have to go. Bye, dear diary.

Monday, October 10, 2016

I have not received any calls from my parents about the matter of Pranav yet. I mean, they did call that day, but we had a normal conversation as usual. I don't know if Kirti had told them about Pranav yet or if my parents are playing smart with me by not asking me anything. Whatever it is, I am glad I am still here studying and enjoying my life with freedom. I don't want to go back home and start spending my further life with some other guy. I don't want that at any cost, and I pray that it never happens.

Things are going great between Pranav and me. We are getting more and more crazy about each other. He is such a great boyfriend, but at times I don't know what happens to him. Maybe he gets his mood swings. A few days back, we went to watch the "Udta Punjab" movie at PVR Sangam. It's been a few minutes since the movie started, Pranav started kissing me. Publicly kissing was not a big deal in cinema halls for me, so we kissed and made out for a few minutes. While kissing, he wrapped his arm around me and began to touch my breasts. It felt good. I didn't stop him and let him please me. But slowly, he lowered his arm and tried to put his hand inside my jeans. I stopped him then. I told him I didn't want to do this in public. But he didn't listen to me. While ignoring my words, he placed his right hand on my mouth, so I couldn't shout, and put his other hand inside my panties. He began to enter his finger in my vagina, which I felt disgusting as my periods were on. When I couldn't take it anymore, I pulled his hand out of my jeans and left the cinema hall sobbing. A few minutes later, he came out of the hall with rage showing all over his face. He came toward me and slapped me twice. The slaps made my vision foggy. I faltered a little and fainted on the floor, losing control all over my body.

I got my consciousness back when someone poured ice-cold water on my face. The water helped, and I opened my eyes partially. There I saw Pranav panicking and trying to wake me up. He kept apologizing for what he did and mumbled, 'Sorry, baby. I don't know why I did that. Wake up. Please wake up.' His words helped a little, and finally, I woke up. All the people surrounding us stared at us with their suspicious eyes while figuring out what happened. Tears were rolling from Pranav's eyes while looking at my condition, but I just ignored him and went out of there. What would I have done? How can he slap me in front of everyone? I was furious at him for hitting me and didn't talk to him the next day. Later after college, when Gita and I were returning to our hostel, he came to speak to me. He told me how sorry he was about what happened between us and promised he would never slap me again in the future. Looking at him begging to get me back made my heart melt.

Dear diary, I might not be able to write to you daily, so please don't get mad at me. Today we have received our Minor exams schedule, and my first exam is on the following Monday. I don't know how I am going to pass my exams. I have been too busy spending time with Pranav and enjoying my love life. You won't believe that from the past week, I haven't even touched a single book. But now I have to study as I don't have any other option. I don't want to give my parents any chance to get disappointed. My Engineering Mathematics–1 textbook is currently opened in front of me, to which I am not that much familiar as I am opening it for the first time. All the theorems and questions are making no sense to me. Now, I realize how Ishaan Awasthi from the movie "Taare Zameen Par" would have felt when he tried to study. I don't know how I will pass my exams, but I have to at any cost. Now I am going to Gita's room. She told me she would help me to cram all these theorems. Yes, we cram everything. Our professors also used to do the same in their childhood. After all, they were also students like us at some point in their life. See you soon, dear diary. Bye.

Monday, October 17, 2016

I am so happy today. I just came from college after attending my first minor exam of Engineering Mathematics–1. I have attempted all the questions, but sure about only three out of four. I think I am going to score good marks in today's exam. Without Gita, it wouldn't have been possible. She helped me to cram all the essential theorems. She also taught me how to solve the questions which were marked important by our mathematics professor. After today's exam, I have the confidence that all my other exams will be good. After dinner today, I will be going to Gita's room to study. She told me she would be helping me with other exams also because that's what is best for me, as I can't learn on my own. I think Gita is my lucky charm, and until she is around me, I can never score fewer marks.

Well, unlike my exams, my relationship isn't going that great. As you know, my exams are going on, and I have to study hard for them, but Pranav can't understand this. He wants to spend time with me. I told him many times to wait for my exams to get over, but he is behaving too immaturely. He wants to be with me all the time, and when he doesn't get to be, he gets mad at me. Yesterday, he even cursed at me as well. I do not know how to make him understand getting good marks is also essential. After all, after completing my degree, I have to get a job, and good multinational companies look for students with exceptional academic records. They won't even give a single chance to average ones by letting them sit in company placements. I don't want to be in that situation, so I have to work hard from the first semester. But he won't understand and behaves like a child. I was studying in the university's library when Pranav called me, and my phone was not on silent mode. It rang with a loud ringtone, and in a hurry, I ended his call. But he thought I hung up on him, and that made him mad at me. After that, he started calling me nonstop. He did not stop until I gave up, and finally, I had to pick his call as I didn't have any other choice. Then he cursed me on the call. I can't even speak the things he said to me on the call, as they were so vulgar. He came to meet me outside the library and apologized for his behavior. I have forgiven him, thinking maybe he got one of his mood swings, which he's getting these days.

I am going to have lunch. I don't know when I will make another entry as you know, I am swamped these days. See you soon, Dear diary.

Bye.

Wednesday, October 26, 2016

Why God? Why does it have to happen to me? What bad have I done to you or anyone? Was it written in my destiny to happen, or was it me who made it happen when I came into a relationship with Pranav? My body is still hurting a lot. Every part of my body is sore and making it fiendishly difficult for me to even move. Today, our exams are finally over. Thanks to Gita for helping me cram through all the exams. She is a great teacher and makes you understand all the concepts in a pretty straightforward manner. I am lucky to have a friend like her. But I can't say the same for Pranav, and I won't. After all, he is a maniac.

In the afternoon, I came out early from the examination hall, as I knew the answer to almost all the questions asked. I stood outside the entrance for a few minutes waiting for Gita. But when she didn't come, I called Pranav to know where he was so we could meet. For the past few days, he was asking me, 'I want to meet you. When are your exams getting over? I want you very badly, baby.' and whatnot. So, I called him, and he picked the call on the second ring.

'Baby, where are you? My exams are over now. Now I am free and all yours.'

'Fine. I am coming to you. Just tell me, where are you right now?'

'I am standing outside of Examination Hall 4, third floor. Come, fast, baby. My stomach is making weird sounds as I am famished.' I ended the call. He came after a few minutes and then together we went to have lunch at the campus canteen. Pranav ordered two Masala Dosa, which was my favorite.

'Baby, for the first time since we are in a relationship, you ordered my favorite dish. Why is that? Are you just trying to show your love for me, or something else is going on in your mind?'

'Nothing like that. I was missing you for the past few days, so I thought about ordering your favorite dish. Just wanted to make you happy. Why? Is it that terrible to order the dish which your girlfriend likes the most?'

'Aww…No baby. I am happy you did that. You know, I haven't had hearty food since my exams started. Today, I am going to eat all I want.'

'Sure, baby. Eat whatever you want to eat, as later we are going to my flat. I have a surprise planned for you there.'

'What? At your flat? Why baby? What have you planned for me? So, this is the reason you are behaving too nice.'

'Baby, it is a surprise. If I tell you in advance, then it will not be any more of a surprise.' Pranav looked straight into my eyes. After finishing the Dosa's, Pranav paid the shopkeeper, and we walked to his flat. We had to walk for fifteen minutes to reach his flat. He took out the key of the door from his wallet and unlocked the main gate. When the door opened, he gestured to me to enter inside. Looking at him, I went in, and later, he also came and finally locked the main door from inside.

'So, what is the surprise, baby? Where is my surprise? I can't wait for it anymore. Please give it to me now.'

'You have to wait for it a little more. It would be the best surprise ever given by anyone to you.'

'Fine. I will wait. Where is the washroom? I have to use it,' I asked. He pointed to his left toward the bathroom. I went to pee there and came out after a few minutes. But when I came out, Pranav was not there.

'Baby, where are you?' I shouted in amazement.

'I am in the bedroom. Unpacking the surprise for you. Wait for a few minutes, and then you can have your gift,' Pranav shouted from the bedroom. At that time, I didn't know after this moment that my life will not be going to be the same anymore. If I had known, then I would have exited from there at the moment only. But they say things that are supposed to happen, they definitely happen. You can't run from them. They just happen, and you must face their consequences. I roamed for a few seconds in Pranav's flat to pass my time. I checked his kitchen, which was dirty like a dumpster. I can't believe how someone can even think of cooking food at a place like that. Then I went to the lobby and checked his book collections. He had a lot of books, which I wanted to read, but haven't bought them yet. When I was going through his books, I found two envelopes on the book rack. On the outer body of both the envelope's Primus Super Specialty Hospital, Delhi was written. I thought maybe they were some types of reports, and I was right. When I opened the first envelope, it had Pranav's fracture report, which he had some days earlier. But when I opened the second envelope, I went into shock. It was a report from Dr. Ajay Thakur, that same doctor whom we met in the hospital, whom Pranav didn't recognize at that time.

I read the report with stalking eyes. Dissociative identity disorder (DID) was written in bold letters and had a list of prescribed medicines. Mr. Pranav Sharma was written in the patent name field. Looking at the report made no sense to me, as I didn't know at that time what Dissociative identity disorder is. With curiosity, I took out my smartphone to check about it on Google. After typing the disorder name, I pressed the search button. As soon as I pressed the button, a lot of information was shown on the phone screen, and I began to read it aloud. 'Dissociative identity disorder (DID) , previously known as multiple personality disorder (MPD) , is a mental disorder characterized by the maintenance of at least two distinct and relatively enduring personality states. The disorder is accompanied by memory gaps beyond what would be explained by ordinary forgetfulness.' Reading it shook my mind. I wasn't able to comprehend what my eyes were showing to me.

Suddenly, out of nowhere, I felt like I was going to faint. Controlling myself, I sat on the bed. Things started making sense to me one by one. Why Pranav has his mood swings, why he forgets about things, his anger management issue now made perfect sense to me. Just then, Pranav shouted from the room.

'Come inside, baby. Come fast.' I don't know why, but hearing his voice scared the hell out of me. I tried to move my body but failed to do so. It felt like someone glued me to the bed. After taking some long breaths, I regained my consciousness and stood up. I walked to the room with the envelope still in my hand. When I went in, Pranav was lying on the bed all naked. He had not even his briefs on. I just stood there and looked at Pranav with my stalking eyes out of amazement. He also did the same. But when he saw me holding the envelope, he stood up from the bed in a hurry and came toward me to grab the envelope. He took the envelope and the report from my hand. He glared at the reports for a few seconds, and then I don't know what happened to him. Out of nowhere, he began to behave weirdly and began mumbling gibberish.

'Aarohi, please get out of here. Please leave from here till you have time. I can't control him for much longer.'

'Control who? What are you saying, Pranav? Are you okay?'

'The other Pranav...' he spoke a bit and stopped in between without completing the sentence. Then he just stared at me while making a blank face and finally sat on the bed still.

'So, what do we have here? Finally, I got my chance to meet the one and only Aarohi Aggarwal.'

'What? What are you saying, Pranav? What is happening to you? Do you want me to call the ambulance?'

'No. There is no need to call the ambulance for me. Maybe you need an ambulance after I am done with you.'

'What? What do you mean by that?' I said just when Pranav stood up and grabbed my neck.

'No need to make a scene. I promise I will be gentle with you. The other Pranav doesn't like to see beautiful girls like you in pain. Now be still, and let's get over with it,' he said and threw me on the bed. I tried to move but failed as his grip was too tight.

'Why are you doing this to me? Pranav, I love you, but that doesn't mean you can do whatever you like with me. You are hurting me. Let me go now. STOP IT,' I shouted, but he ignored my words and removed my jeans. In no time, he entered inside me, which gave me nothing other than pain. I tried to shout, but he had placed his hand on my face, so no words came out of it.

'Do you like it, baby? If you want, I can be a little gentler. Anything for you, my love.'

'What the hell is wrong with you,' I shouted while crying and pushed him away from me. As soon as I got out of his grip, I picked a flower vase from the side of the bed and banged it on Pranav's head. It made him unconscious, and he collapsed on the floor. I wore my clothes back again. A few moments later, he woke up and walked to me.

'Baby, why are you crying? What happened? I thought you were also enjoying it.' he said, but in response, I slapped him and ran out of the room. In a hurry, I picked up my backpack, opened the lock, and left from there. Later I went to my hostel and locked myself in the room. Pranav is a psycho. Why didn't I get to know about it earlier? I can't believe I am dating a crazy boy like him. Currently, I am in my bed, still trying to collect my broken pieces. The pain is not letting me write, but I must complete writing today's entry. I have decided I will not date Pranav anymore. He is dead for me. I don't even want to see his face anymore. I don't know what I could do the next time I see him. I can even kill him for what he did to me today. So, the best thing for both of us is to keep away from each other as much as possible. My hand is shivering from the pain right now. I can't write anymore. Bye, Dear

Diary.

Tuesday, November 1, 2016

Pranav and I have broken up since the incident happened at his flat. We haven't talked to each other since then. When I came back to my hostel that day, Pranav called me multiple times, but I didn't pick his call. He also kept calling me for almost a week, and I had to answer his call as I knew if I didn't talk with him, he would not stop. After all, he is the most stubborn guy I've ever met in my life.

'Baby, why were you not picking my call? You didn't even meet me after that day. I told you I am sorry about what happened between us.'

'Shut up, Pranav. I don't want to be with you anymore. Do you even remember what you did to me that day or even forgot that also as always?'

'I remember everything, baby. I had sex with the love of my life, and that's you. I remember this. How can you even though I can forget about it?'

'No, you fucking bastard. You didn't make love to me. Instead, you raped me. I told you many times I am not ready for sex yet, but yet you forced yourself on me to sleep with you.'

'What are you talking about, baby? I forced nothing on you, ever. When you came with me to my flat, I thought you also wanted the same. I thought you too wanted to be intimate with me.'

'Got to hell and take your medicines at a time. You are going weirder day by day. You psycho. From now on, don't try to call me and get the hell out of my life.'

'Wait, baby. Please don't say this…' he tried to speak, but I hung up on him in-between his sentence. This person not only gets mood swings but, instead, is also a maniac. I can't believe I dated him. Whatever happened, it is my past. From now on, I will have to learn how to live without him. I took an oath that day that I will never talk to him and not to go back to him. Even after all this drama, I was only able to keep the commitment till today and finally called him. I had to call him after what I got to know, and this time also it was all because of his silly mistake.

Today we got the result of our minor exams, and I scored much better in the exams than expected. I scored over fifteen out of twenty marks in all the exams, and in Engineering Mathematics-1 I don't know how, but I scored twenty. I mean, I studied hard for it, but I didn't think I would score the full marks. It all happened only because of one person, my friend Gita. Without her, it never would have been possible. After all, she is the one who taught me how to cram things. I thanked her and asked if she is willing to teach me in upcoming exams also and to which she said, 'of course I will do. We are friends, and friends do all sorts of things. I would love to help you.' Hearing her, I realized I am fortunate to have a friend like her.

I don't know if it was my excitement or something I ate, but out of nowhere, my stomach began to hurt. I tried to keep myself calm, but it didn't help. Instead, the pain kept increasing with every passing second. When I couldn't bear it anymore, I told Gita about it, sitting just next to me. Listening to me, she stood up in between ongoing lectures and talked about my condition with Professor Suresh. He told Gita to take me to a hospital as soon as possible. As he thought, it can be something severe.

Gita and I left the classroom and went to Primus Super Specialty Hospital. In the hospital, we met Dr. Sunita Singh, who was supposed to be the best Gynecologist in the whole city. She told us that I have to do an ultrasound, and after that, only she can tell us why I am having stomach pain. Following her order, we went to the ultrasound center and got my ultrasound scanning done. After collecting the reports of the scanning, we went to show them to Dr. Sunita Singh. We were sitting in her room in front of her. She kept staring at the report and didn't speak a single word for a few minutes. She just kept her lips sealed. When I couldn't wait anymore, and out of curiosity and worry, I asked her, 'Doctor, is there something wrong with the report.'

'My dear, I don't know what to tell you. According to the reports, you are pregnant. It looks like you are 12 days pregnant.'

'What? Am I pregnant? How is it possible? I haven't even been physical with anyone for many days. What if my parents get to know about my condition? They will kill me.' I panicked and started crying.

'Don't cry beta. I am just telling you what the ultrasound report is showing.'

'So, what do I do now? I can abort it if I want to, right?' I mumbled.

'Yes, you can. But for that, any member of your family must have to be with you at the time of the abortion. This is the way things happen in our hospital. It is our policy.' Just when she said the "family" word, I felt a shiver deep down my spine. I felt slight drowsiness in my head and I again panicked.

'Doctor, Can I get some water?' I mumbled in a broken tone. Listening to me, Dr. Sunita handed me a glass full of water, and I drank it with small sips. The water helped, and I gestured to Gita that let's leave now. After greeting Dr. Sunita, we went out of the room and walked to the hospital exit. But again, out of nowhere, Dr. Ajay Gupta appeared there, the same as the last time. Looking at him, I thought he doesn't have any work to do, or he is so lonely that he roams around the hospital to hunt his previous patients so that he could talk with them.

'Hello. How are you, and how is Pranav doing? Is he taking his medicine at the time?'

'I am good, and he is also fine. Yes, I suppose he is taking his medicine at the time. Dr. Ajay, if you don't mind, then can you tell us what is wrong with Pranav? I mean, I know about his condition, but as you are his doctor, so can you tell us about it in much more detail.'

'Off course beta. Let's go to my office and have some tea. There, I will tell you all about Pranav's case,' Dr. Ajay Thakur said and walked to his office. We followed him as his shadow and after walking for a minute we finally reached his office. He ordered three cups of tea and eventually began to explain Pranav's case.

'Pranav's parents came to me when he was just ten years old and told me that their son has mood swings quite often. At one moment, he would be doing perfectly fine, and at another, he began to cry his lungs out. So, listening to them, I asked if they could bring Pranav to the hospital, so I can meet him personally and learn about his behavior,' Dr. Ajay said and stopped as the tea had just arrived. We began to drink our tea with small sips, and after having a few slurps, he spoke again. 'So, the next day, they arrived at my clinic with Pranav with them. Initially, he was terrified of me as we were only meeting for the first time. But as the days passed, he felt comfortable with me and began to share his feelings with me.

I analyzed his behavior for a few days. Finally, I got to know he has two separate personalities. In scientific terms, he is suffering from Dissociative identity disorder (DID) , which is also known as multiple personality disorder. The one personality is the one which was Pranav's and the other which is the opposite to his actual's. I tried to speak to his other self many times and then got to know he calls himself "the other Pranav". I asked him why he calls himself that, and in response, he said he is the other part of Pranav's conscience, so he calls himself the other Pranav. He also told one day he will learn how to control the real Pranav and destroy his life. Eventually, he said he will kill the real self of Pranav and will take the place of it. As he said, he somehow did and found a way to suppress his actual self. He does that by giving intentional mood swings to Pranav, which helps him to take control over Pranav's true self,' Dr. Ajay said and again began to drink his tea. After finishing our tea, we thanked him for his time and left for our hostel.

Thursday, November 10, 2016

Since the day I got to know I am pregnant, my entire life has turned upside down. I can't focus on anything these days. The news of my pregnancy is eating me from inside like a beetle eats the wood. I can't decide what to do with my unborn child. I have the abortion option, but that also I couldn't do. What if my parents get to know about abortion from somewhere? This thought was coming to my mind, again and again, and scaring the hell out of me. I am pretty sure if this happens, they will marry me to some guy, and then I have to spend my entire life hearing his tantrums and pleasing him, which I don't want at my cost. So finally, I made up my mind to get aborted. A few days back, Gita and I went to meet Dr. Sanjana Panday. I told her that I wanted to abort my child. While Dr. Sanjana was preparing for the abortion, I panicked, and we left the clinic without getting the abortion done. I wanted to abort my unborn child, but I couldn't. Maybe it's my motherly instinct, or maybe it's just that I don't want to be the murderer of an unborn child.

From the moment I got the news of my pregnancy, I am trying to call Pranav, but he is not answering my call anymore. I know I told him myself not to call me anymore, but if I call him, then he doesn't have to pick up that I haven't told him. Calling him after waking up became a ritual of my life. These days, as soon as I wake up, I pick my smartphone and call him. But in the answer, I hear only the preloaded voice of some lady saying, 'The number is not reachable.' But today maybe was my lucky day. When I woke up, I called him as usual, but no computer lady spoke; instead, it began to ring. After two long rings, he finally picked up the call.

'Now, what do you want from me? I thought we were broken up. Am I right?' Pranav asked in a flat tone.

'Yes, we were, but not anymore. I was trying to call you for many days, but I don't remember you picking my call. Are you so angry with me that you do not even want to hear my voice anymore?'

'No, it's not like that. You can't understand what's going inside me. I know what happened between us was wrong, but mother promise, I haven't done it intentionally. I never wanted to hurt you in any way. I love you so much you can't even believe it.'

'I believe it. Now, I know baby, why were you behaving so weirdly, and why did you get those mood swings. I have met Dr. Ajay Thakur, and he told me everything about your condition. Also, I know about "the other Pranav".'

'Baby, I am so sorry I came into a relationship with you and ruined your life. I wanted to tell you about my condition for quite a long time, but couldn't gather the courage to confront you. I though, if I tell you the truth, you will leave me and that I didn't want to at any cost. If you don't want to talk to me anymore, I understand and will respect your decision.'

'I love you so much, baby. I want you in my life, and if I don't get you, I will die. You know I am having your child inside me?'

'What? My child? But we haven't been physical for many days? So, how is it even possible?'

'When you told me, you had planned a surprise for me at your flat and tricked me into coming to your flat and what happened that day, it is the result of that, I suppose. You forced me, or I say "the other Pranav" forced me to have sex with him, and he didn't make you wore a condom. So, now I am pregnant.'

'Yes, now I remember. He must have done it intentionally so that he can add one more thing to my suffering. I don't know why he is doing this to me. I can't take it anymore baby.'

'Don't cry baby. Now I know what you are going through, we will find a way to get rid of that bastard. Listen, I want to meet you very badly. Tell me where we can meet.'

'Fine, baby. You can come to my flat. My roommate is going to his home for his sister's wedding. I am all alone at my flat.'

'Okay then. I will come tomorrow to your flat. Love you baby. Bye,' I said and ended the call. After talking with Pranav, I feel like an immense burden is lifted from my head. You know, dear diary, I am going to ask Pranav to marry me tomorrow. If he said yes, then the entire problem is going to get solved on its own. After marriage, my parents can't make me abort the child, and they have to accept our wedding even if they don't want to. I hope everything goes as I imagined it to go. Now I am starving and going to have lunch. I missed breakfast as I overslept and didn't even go to college today. See you soon, dear diary. Bye.

Friday, November 11, 2016

I am done. I don't want to live anymore, so I have decided to end my life. There is nothing more left in it for me to live. This will be my last entry in this diary. I know it's a big thing to say and to do, but I don't have any other option because what Pranav did to me today has crushed my soul, and my love for him is all gone. I thought there was a chance we could be together again, and if everything happens the way I wanted it to, eventually we will get married. But when your boyfriend is some sort of psycho and suffering from a severe disease, it is just not possible.

Today, I went to his flat as we planned to meet there. I knocked on the main door of his flat, but he didn't open it. After knocking for two more consecutive times, I heard the sound of approaching footsteps, and finally, Pranav opened the door. We hugged for a few seconds while standing at the door, and then he asked me to come inside, and I went in. He made me sit in the bedroom, and he went to the kitchen. As soon as he went there, I heard him shouting from the kitchen.

'What will you have? Coffee or Tea?' Pranav asked.

'Coffee is fine,' I said and went silent. To pass the time, I began to analyze Pranav's room. It was just the same as earlier and had no significant changes. I roamed in his room and looked here and there. A few minutes later, he entered the bedroom holding two cups of freshly made coffee. He handed me one cup and gestured for me to sit. I sat next to him on the bed.

'I am so sorry baby, for what I made you go through. Such a pathetic boyfriend I am. I deserve to rot in hell for my doings.'

'Don't say this. We both know you haven't done anything intentionally. The other Pranav made you do it to me.'

'Yes, that other Pranav made me do it. So, are you going to forgive me for my actions, which I have done in the past? And for those too, which I am going to commit today.'

'What? What are you saying? What are you going to do today?'

'Sorry, baby. He made me ask you to come here once again. I am under his control and did what he asked me to do. If I don't follow his order, he hurts me,' said Pranav while sobbing and lifted his shirt sleeve to show me his wrist. There were many scratches on his inner wrist like someone tried to cut it. 'When I don't do what he asks me to do, then he gives me a cut here' Pranav mumbled, sobbing, and pointed at the cuts on his wrist.

'Why didn't you tell me about it earlier? We could have gone to Dr. Ajay to talk about this,' I spoke, and just then, my vision went blurry.

My head began to spin in circles, and it made me dizzy. 'Did you give me something in the coffee?' I mumbled and stared at Pranav's face in blurry vision. Listening to me, he grabbed my head and began to caress it like I was a newly born baby.

'Shh…Shh…Everything is fine. You just go to sleep and leave the other things to me. I will correct everything now. You don't worry and just go to sleep.' Pranav closed my eyes with his fingers.

'Wake up. Wake up, Aarohi. No need to sleep anymore. Everything went just perfectly as I supposed it to go. Now, will you open your eyes yourself, or do you want me to open them for you?' Pranav shouted in my ears. His sharp voice went to my ears and made me uneasy. Finally, I opened my eyes partially. I saw Pranav standing in front of me in the blurred vision, shaking me and trying to wake me up.

'What did you do to me? Why is my stomach hurting so much?' I screamed in pain.

'It will hurt for a few hours, and then the pain will go away. I removed something from inside you which was not supposed to be there.'

'What? Wait for a second, did you operate on me? Did you just abort me all by yourself?'

'So, what did you think when you came here? I didn't ask you to come here just to sleep with you. I mean, I have already done that. Pranav wanted to do so, but I didn't let him. I only let him sleep only for a single time with the same girl, and then he has to find another one. This is how I like it.'

What are you saying, Pranav? I know you are somewhere in there. If you concentrate, I know you can stop him from controlling you. Listen to my voice and try to focus on regaining your consciousness.'

'What are you doing, bitch? Do you think it will work? Do you think that…?' Pranav said, but stopped in between without completing his sentence and finally sat on the bed next to me. It took him a few minutes to get back to his conscience, but he finally got it back. 'Why are you lying here like this, baby? Did we have sex?'

'No. The other Pranav aborted me all by himself. I don't even know how he did it. I mean, you are not a medical student, so how is it even possible?'

'What the fuck? What are you saying? It is possible, baby. I used to dissect frogs in my childhood just for fun. He is capable of anything.'

'I am not feeling well. Baby, please take me to the hospital. I don't want to die here like this. I am feeling like vomiting,' I mumbled while sobbing and threw up on the floor. Looking at my failing health, Pranav took me to Primus Super Specialty Hospital. There we met Dr. Sunita Singh, and when she looked at my wound from the operation, she said it was just perfect. It seems like the work of some professional, she said and prescribed some medicines for me. After leaving the hospital, I asked Pranav to drop me at my hostel. He did as told and finally dropped me.

I don't know why, but I felt like meeting Charu as soon as I entered the hostel. Listening to the voice of my heart, I went to her room. She opened the door on the first knock and went blank when she saw me standing there. She just stared at me with her mouth wide open in amazement.

'I need you, Charu. Please help me. I can't trust any other more than you,' I mumbled.

'Why are you crying, Aarohi? What happened to you? Your face is also looking paler than usual.'

'First, I need to lie down for a few seconds. Do you mind if I?'

'No. Come inside.' Charu said and made me lie down on her bed.

'Now tell me what is wrong? Is your health okay?'

'Nothing is okay. I don't want to live anymore. Kill me, Charu. Please kill me.'

'Why are you saying this nonsense? What happened to you?' Charu asked. But in response, I pulled her face close to me and kissed her. In reply, she took a few seconds to realize what just happened, and then she also began to kiss me. We made out for a few minutes, and then she moved her hand into my panties. But when she started to move her finger, I got my conscience back and finally stopped her.

'I am sorry I came here. We were not supposed to do this. This doesn't seem right.' I said and stood up.

'No, please stay. Please stay for me, Aarohi,' Charu requested.

'Sorry, Charu. I want to, but I can't,' I said and left from there in a hurry. I don't know why I made out with Charu. I mean, I am not physically attracted to her, but still, I kissed her. Maybe I was feeling low at the moment and wanted to be with someone. But these things don't matter anymore. Now, I came too far from these things. I can't live with these people anymore. I can't live with myself. My wound from the operation is hurting a lot, so now I can't write further. I suppose our journey was meant to be until this moment only. So, bye-bye, dear diary. But this time I can't even say I will see you soon because I will not. If anyone finds this diary after my death, please don't read it, but you can keep it to yourself. There is no need to create more chaos in people's lives, as everyone is already suffering somehow. Now I have to go and get dead. Goodbye.

CHAPTER 19

Kirti Speaks I

I still can't believe that Aarohi is dead. My heart is just not ready to accept the truth that she is not with us anymore. She was one of my best friends, despite our differences. It's not that I forget the moments we spent with each other and cherished together. We had spent each moment together when we were children, but later things changed. When my parents started to compare my dark complexion with Aarohi's mesmerizing beauty and fair skin, I began to hate her. We even stopped talking and seeing each other, but the truth is I never stopped thinking about her. I only pretended to hate her because I just wanted her to go away from me so that the taunts of my parents about my complexion stops.

Finally, my dream came true. When I got selected for a scholarship for my higher studies, I had to shift to Bangalore. It felt great when I realized I no longer have to listen to my parents' taunts about my dark complexion. But when I moved to Bangalore, I don't know why, but I started to miss Aarohi. I was so used to being around her all the time that I didn't realize she had become an irreplaceable part of my life. I started stalking Aarohi daily on Instagram and read her poetry, which she uploaded there.

Everything was going great until I received a call from Suman aunty, Aarohi's mom. She told me Aarohi got admission to the University of Delhi and went there to study Computer Science and Engineering. Out of curiosity, I couldn't stop myself and ended up calling Aarohi. I asked her if she had a boyfriend, and she told me about Pranav.

Listening to her, I told her to wait and watch what I will do now. At that time, I only thought a little and mumbled whatever came to my head. What would I have done? After all, I had to justify my hate for her. So, I just said that to play with her. It was not like I was going to tell her parents.

A few days after I talked with Aarohi when I received a call from Suman aunty saying that Aarohi was dead. She told me that Aarohi committed suicide by hanging with a rope. The word "Suicide" gave me a chill deep down my spine, and I began to sweat in no time. After disconnecting the call, I thought, what if Aarohi committed suicide just because of me? She would have thought I would tell her parents about Pranav. She went scared of facing her parents, and she finally ended her life and committing suicide. That day, I couldn't sleep the entire night because of guilt. It was eating me from the inside, and finally, I decided to visit Aarohi's hostel. I thought maybe she left a note or letter. So, I went to her hostel the very next day.

I stood outside Aarohi's hostel room and looked at the giant lock hanging on the door with disappointment. I didn't know what to do next, so I turned around and began to walk back home. Just then I heard someone calling me.

'Hey. Who are you? What are you doing here? Don't you know you can't move inside this boundary? This is a crime scene.' The girl pointed to the boundary made by the police.

'I am sorry. I am Aarohi's cousin, Kirti Aggarwal. I just came here to check if she left any note or letter before committing suicide. I know for sure she can't just kill herself without even leaving any note behind.'

'Oh, so you are Kirti. Aarohi told me about you and the history between you two. She did leave a note, but it is in police custody now. But I can help you to know what she wrote in it.'

'Oh really? Yes, please show it to me if you have it. Hang on, you

just told me that the letter is in police custody, so how will you show it to me, and who are you? Do you know Aarohi?'

'My name is Charu. I knew Aarohi very well. Aarohi and I were roommates, and she was my classmate also.' Charu pulled her smartphone out from her jeans pocket. After clicking a few times on the phone's screen, she handed me her phone. I took it, and just when I looked at it, I went into shock. It was the picture of Aarohi's last letter which she had left. I read the letter with a broken heart and began sobbing. But after reading the letter, I felt something suspicious about it. The handwriting in the letter was very different from Aarohi's. I had known Aarohi for my entire childhood and can tell the difference between her and other people's handwriting. But at that time, I ignored it as there were other things in my mind to worry about.

'Listen, Charu, I wanted to check Aarohi's room for something, but it is locked. Is there any way we can get the key?'

'It might be possible, but I can't give you any surety about it. We will have to ask the warden to give us the key.'

'So, let's go to her office and ask for the key.' Charu and I started walking toward the warden's office. I followed her like her shadow, and we reached the warden's office in no time.

'Hello miss. This is Aarohi's cousin sister, Kirti. That Aarohi who committed suicide yesterday. She wants to look into Aarohi's room to check if she had left any note behind her.'

'Beta, I can't do that. If I let you go in there, then my job will be in jeopardy. Try to understand,' said the warden.

'Please, mam, let me have a look in her room, just for a few minutes. I beg you. Please let me see my dead sister's room.' I started sobbing.

'Stop crying, beta. I can't see anyone crying like this. I will give you the key to her room. But you have to promise you will give back the key

to me in five minutes. Is it fine?'

'Yes yes. I will. You are doing me a huge favor. Take these five hundred rupees for the help. Buy something good for you and your children,' I said while handing a crisp note of five hundred rupees. She didn't hesitate and took it while smiling.

'Here is the key. Now go and check her room. But please return the key in five minutes. I can't afford to lose my job at any cost.' She handed me the key with a worried face.

'Sure mam. We will be back in a few minutes,' I said, and we both walked to Aarohi's room. I handed Charu the key, and she opened the lock. After removing the lock from the door, she pushed the door, and it opened with ease. We both went inside. The room was all empty except for a bed.

'Oh, there is nothing in here. What can we possibly find here?' Charu said, but I ignored her and began to look for what I came for. But what Charu said was true. There was nothing in the room except darkness and emptiness. Despite that, I began to look, as I was positive that I would find something. I opened Aarohi's cupboard, and it was also empty. There were just a few novels and textbooks in there. I took all the books out from the closet and started going through them one by one. After checking the first, second, and finally the third book, I gave up and threw the books back in the cupboard. Just then, I saw a notebook in there. I grabbed it and opened it, and went into shock. Charu looked at my blank face and realized I must have found something important and walked to me.

'Didi, what is this? Is it a diary?' Charu asked with amazement.

'Yes, it is, I suppose. It is Aarohi's diary. She must have started writing a journal after she came here, as the diary's initial entry is of 29 August,' I spoke.

'Can I have her diary? I want to know if Aarohi wrote something

about me in it. I promise I will return it to you after reading.'

'No, I am sorry. I can't give this to you. This is the most important evidence in Aarohi's case. I have to take this to the police.' I lied.

'Fine. Do as you want, bitch.' Charu left the room cursing me. As soon as she left, I placed the diary in my handbag and locked the room in a hurry so no one could see me. After closing the room, I went to the warden's office and returned her the key, and came back to my house.

CHAPTER 20

Kirti Speaks II

When I reached my house, I went directly to my room and locked the room. My mother knocked many times on the door, but I had locked the door from inside. After knocking a few times, she realized I was not in the mood to meet her, so she finally stopped hitting. I sat on my bed and took some long breaths to calm myself. A few seconds later, when I felt like myself, I took out Aarohi's diary from my handbag and started reading it. It took me less than an hour to complete it. When I read the last lines of Aarohi's diary saying, 'There is no need to create more chaos in people's lives, as everyone is already suffering somehow. Now I have to go and get dead. Goodbye.' Tears rolled out of my eyes. I started crying like a kid. Millions of thoughts sprouted in my mind at that moment, but I couldn't do anything. I mean, Aarohi was already dead, and there was nothing I could do to bring her back to life. But I wanted to avenge Aarohi. That bastard pushed my cousin so much that she finally committed suicide. I couldn't let him go that easily. So, I made a plan. A plan that could destroy that bastard's life and help Aarohi's soul to rest in peace.

I went out of my room and told my parents the truth behind Aarohi's death. My father wanted me to take the diary to the police. But when I told them about my plan for Pranav they freaked out.

'Are you out of your mind? Do you even realize what you are saying? What if he gets to know the truth behind you marrying him? Mom asked in a serious tone.

'What do you want me to do, Mom? Tell me. What if I take Aarohi's

diary to the police and Pranav bribes them not to drag him in the case? You know he is a bestselling author. He will push his limits to save his name.' After convincing them for a few minutes, they realized what I had planned for that scum is much better than just rotting in jail. I mean, he will go to jail eventually, but not yet. First, I have to make his life hell as he did with my cousin's.

Later we talked to Aarohi's parents, and I convinced them too. At that time, the news of Aarohi's suicide was selling like hot cake, so I wanted to wait until everything settled down. I also had to complete my graduation before executing my plan. That day I called my best friend Anuj Singh, who was working in a startup, DreamShaddi.com. I told him to create a profile for me on the website and told him he has to optimize the website in such a way that if any person of the name "Pranav Sharma" sign-up there, my profile must come into his match. He said that it is a tricky thing to do, but he will tell his team members to work on it.

After approximately four years, when Mr. Pranav Sharma finally signed up on DreamShaddi.com, my profile showed up in his matches, and he texted me just as we thought he would do. When I received his text that day, I cried out of happiness. After waiting for all these years, things finally started happening the way I planned. I arranged a meeting with his family at my house, and my parents selected him as the best suitable groom for me as planned.

When our marriage got fixed, I began to chat with him, so that he didn't doubt me even for a second. As the days passed, we came close and even started sexting, which was not a part of the plan. I started developing some feelings for him, but when I felt that, I used to read Aarohi's diary, to make those feelings disappear. Days kept on passing and one day we finally got married, and I came to his home. On the first day, I lied and made an excuse to my mother-in-law that I was feeling exhausted and wanted to lie down. She made me sleep in her room, which was what I wanted. I knew that if we slept in one room, he would surely try to get physical with me, which I didn't want yet to happen. When I was lying on the bed that day, I saw Pranav trying to sneak into the room.

The next morning, when I went to Pranav's room, he was mumbling in his sleep. I thought of playing with him, so I began to caress his body and rubbed his crotch. But to my surprise, he began to mumble Aarohi's. I wanted to punch him then and there, but I controlled myself. As it was just the start and I would be getting many more chances to make him suffer for his doings.

On the day of my Mooh dikhai, I intentionally didn't wear my Chooda and went without makeup to attend the ceremony. I knew if I did that, they would think it is an Apshagun, and it is absolutely not good to happen just after marriage. But when Pranav's mother fainted in the ceremony, I felt horrible. After that incident, I decided not to do something like that again. I didn't want to hurt Pranav's parents anymore, so I thought if I take him out from here to Bangalore, that would be best. That way, I would be getting more alone time with him. Finally, I lied to him that I got transferred to Bangalore and wanted him to come with me. He asked his parents about it, and after a lot of convincing, they permitted him to go with me to Bangalore.

When we shifted to Bangalore, I played my next card. I started calling him on our home landline from my office. I used a voice changer application as I didn't want to get caught. At first, he resisted talking. But when I mentioned about Aarohi's diary during one of the calls, the other Pranav came out of his rathole. He threatened to kill me, but I knew he couldn't do that, as I knew he was not the man of his words.

Later, I made him sleep with me, which he was waiting for since we got married. He insisted on wearing a condom, but I forced him not to as planned, and we had sex without it. After some days, as expected, *my health fell, and I began to vomit. When I went to a nearby hospital and met a gynecologist, she told me that I am pregnant. Hearing the news of my pregnancy, Pranav became very happy, but he didn't know at that moment what was going to happen to him in the coming days. I started behaving weirdly as the days passed. I also started to act drunk. Due to this we even had a huge fight a few times. I can't even express how good I felt looking at him begging me to stop drinking, as it was terrible for the baby's health. But he didn't know I was only acting that way. I am not that dumb person who knows she is pregnant and instead drinks.*

When he couldn't take it anymore, he called his parents to come to our flat. I didn't think he would do that, so I had to pull out my master card much earlier than I planned to. The day Pranav's parents came to our flat, I went to a party at my friend's place. The party was just an excuse to get out of the house. My immediate plan was to disappear. I wanted to give him as much pain as I could provide, so I came back to Delhi to my parent's house. I told them to tell Pranav's parents that I was not here, and even hadn't called them for many days.

After eight months from then, I gave birth to my baby daughter at my parent's house. We named her after Aarohi. She is such a cute baby. After giving her birth, I realized how difficult it is for a single mother to take care of the child. So, I decided to execute the final step of the plan for which our family was convinced and was waiting desperately for the past few years. I wrote him a letter telling him that I am perfectly fine, and I wanted to meet him, so he has to fix a meeting for us.

A few days later, I received his letter in which he mentioned his upcoming author interview at Mahatma Public library, and that he wanted to meet me there. After reading his letter, I called Mahatma Public library and told them I was Pranav Sharma's wife, and I am willing to sponsor the whole event of my husband's interview. They agreed to it immediately as it was also good for them to save all their money. I told them not to reveal anything about our conversation to Pranav as I wanted it to be a surprise for him.

Currently, Pranav is in jail, and now I can live my life fully. I feel like an immense burden has been lifted from my shoulder. I finally avenged Aarohi. That scum deserves to rot in jail. It was written in his destiny. Our families feel much better knowing that the murderer of their daughter is now in jail. I decided to visit the prison to see him rotting with my own eyes. I have also decided something else for him, but that I can't tell just now. You all have to wait and will get to know about it very soon.

CHAPTER 21

The Other Pranav Speaks

Fuck you bitch, and I mean it from all my heart. Believe my words. I will kill you Kirti for sure, as soon as I get out of here. I will never forget what people do to me that easily. If you want to live your life peacefully, then make sure they keep me locked up in here.

I have been locked up my entire life being locked up inside Pranav, so this prison is something I can deal with, but Pranav's condition is getting worse day by day. I didn't think he would suffer this much. If I had known, I would have never done anything. I did whatever I had to, to get my revenge. Now looking at Pranav in such awful condition is making me feel guilty. After all, he is me, and I am him. But I can't forget what he did to me. I mean, how can I? I genuinely liked the first girl in my whole life, and he pushed her away from me.

It had been a few days since we joined the University of Delhi to study Mechanical Engineering when I fell in love with a girl. When I looked at her for the first time, my heart skipped a beat. She was one of the two girls who were in our batch. The ratio of boys to girls in our class was 25:2. So, this made those two girls most wanted, and all the boys began to give them attention, thinking maybe they would become friends with them. Both of them were too shy, and they didn't speak much to any boy in our class. They just come to the class to attend the lectures and leave from there as soon as the professor leaves the classroom. I got to know that her name was Gitanjali Ahuja, who I was in love with. She did see me a few times in the class but didn't give me much attention, which I thought she would give. After all, I was good-looking and, on top of that, also a writer. But she never initiated any conversation with me, as this is what girls are taught to do. It is the responsibility of boys to talk first, and this is how this world works. Girls would never come to you to begin the conversation or make the first move unless you are a singer, actor, or, say, a billionaire.

One day, Gitanjali's friend Pooja didn't come to attend the class with her. When I entered the class that day, I saw Gitanjali sitting alone and thought it was a good opportunity to get to know her and be friends with her. I went to her and asked if I could sit next to her. She let me sit next to her. We talked for the whole lecture. But I was only able to dominate Pranav's consciousness for a few minutes, and finally, he took control over me.

'I am so sorry if I said something wrong to you,' said Pranav, worrying thinking maybe the other Pranav had said something wrong to her.

'What are you talking about, Pranav? Why are you saying this? Are you okay?' Gitanjali asked, but Pranav didn't reply and left the class without answering her. I wanted to talk more with her, but I couldn't take control over Pranav's conscience again. As days were passing by, his therapy was working. It was curing him while killing me on the other hand. His relationship with Aarohi was also getting serious day by day. I thought I would lose Gitanjali forever if things kept getting better between Pranav and Aarohi. From that day, I started looking for ways to end Pranav and Aarohi's relationship and secure my future with Gitanjali. But that girl Aarohi was so stubborn that whatever I made Pranav do, didn't affect her even a bit.

I made Pranav get in a fight with a guy and almost made him kill the guy in front of her just because he was kicking Aarohi's shoes from behind. Not only that, I even made him kick Professor Suresh in the stomach, thinking it will freak out Aarohi, and she will leave Pranav, but it too didn't work. They got closer after that day, and finally, Pranav proposed to Aarohi. She, too, accepted the proposal, which made it more difficult for me to meet Gitanjali anymore.

When they went to PVR Sangam to watch the "Udta Punjab" movie, I tried to touch Aarohi inappropriately against her consent. Even I made him slap Aarohi in front of everyone and kept pushing her until they broke up, and finally, I won. I was so happy that day, but my happiness was only a guest for a few days and didn't remain for much longer. I don't know how and why they again patched up and began to date. How can she still be with him after whatever happened between them, I thought, but then I realized love is what keeps them together. If I want to separate them, I have to hit them where it will hurt them the most, i.e., their love for each other. I had to find a way that would change their love for each other into hate.

Days kept passing, and they came closer. I made a plan and somehow convinced Aarohi to come to my flat and raped her. I know it is a cruel thing to do, but what could I have done? I didn't want to lose Gitanjali at any cost and did what I could. But it didn't go how I thought it would, and accidentally I made Aarohi pregnant. I was pretty sure I made Pranav wear a condom, but I was wrong. In excitement, I forgot to wear it and came inside Aarohi, which ultimately made her pregnant. Just like that, I got one more thing to worry about.

One day Pranav was with Aarohi, spending quality time which I hate, of course, and it made us late to attend the lecture. When we entered the classroom during the ongoing lecture, I saw a guy sitting next to Gitanjali. When I moved closer to their bench, I saw that the guy was holding Gitanjali's hand and was caressing it. Looking at them, I don't know what got inside me, and I began to shout and curse at them. The professor made me leave the classroom, and I was suspended for a week. I was so furious that day, I wasn't able to think straight and ended up calling Aarohi and convinced her to meet me at my flat.

I was furious at her that day because I thought whatever happened to me, she was responsible for it. If I can't be with Gitanjali, then I will also not let them be together. I wanted to kill Aarohi, but after thinking a lot, I realized it could create more problems for me later, so I dropped that thought.

When Aarohi came to my flat, I mixed a sleeping pill in her coffee. When she went to deep sleep and lost all her body control, I aborted her child. Pranav used to operate on frogs in the biology labs when he was in school, and that knowledge helped me a lot that day.

A few days later, when I heard the news of Aarohi's suicide, it triggered something inside me. I felt both happy and sad at the same time. I don't know why I felt that way, but I just did. Maybe it was the feelings of Pranav for Aarohi which were still there and affecting me at that time. I was glad when Aarohi died that no one else would get to know what I have done to her. So, to make sure of my innocence, that night, I went to Aarohi's hostel to check if she had left some suicide note or not. If not, then it is my responsibility to leave one to save myself. I thought if I write a note in which Aarohi accepts she was cheating on her boyfriend, i.e., me, and when she confronts me about it, I leave her. She couldn't take it, and the thought of killing herself came to her mind. If I write this, then no one would dare to doubt me. So, I sneaked to her room and left a fake suicide note there.

At that time, I didn't think that the actual truth would come out after four years, and I would get caught in my own web of lies. But it happened, and now I am in this fucking prison. It's not like I am scared to die in jail, but the one thing which I want before it happens is a chance to kill that bitch Kirti. Now it is the only thing I want from God if it exists in reality.

CHAPTER 22

The Darkness Returns

'Aarohi, why did you come here? I told you not to come here anymore. If she sees you here, she will kill us both,' I said worryingly.

'It had been so long since we met. I couldn't control myself and came to meet you today. She will not come, I promise,' Aarohi spoke with surety.

'How can you promise that she won't come here anymore with so much confidence? Have you done something to her?'

'Are you mad, Pranav? I can't even face her, and you are asking if I have done something to her. I only said because I thought she must be sleeping at this time as it's late-night.'

'Oh, okay. Aarohi, I was dying to meet you. I also thought about running from here. But I remembered what your other half would do to us if I left the cell and tried to meet you again. But I am glad you came to see me.' Listening to me, tears came out of Aarohi's eyes. She looked at me with tear-filled eyes. I also began to sob. We tightly hugged each other and finally kissed. Just then, I opened my mouth to speak, but she covered my mouth with her hand.

'Shh… can you hear something?' Aarohi whispered.

'What? What are you talking about? Are you hearing something?' I asked in a low tone and tried to listen to what Aarohi was talking about.

'Can't you hear the sound of someone approaching footsteps toward the cell?'

'Oh, yes. It must be your other half. I told you not to come here. I knew coming here was not a good plan. Aarohi, please go before she comes here.'

'Fine. I am going. Can I get a goodbye kiss?' She made a puppy face.

'Come here.' I pulled her close to me, and finally, we kissed for a few seconds. 'She will be coming here any time now, and I don't want you to get caught. After all, I don't have anyone in my life except you. Please go.' While holding her hand, I walked her to the exit. When we reached the main gate, we could hear the approaching footsteps. In a hurry, Aarohi ran out of the cell but as she jerked her hand away from mine, her golden bracket fell on the ground, and she suddenly stopped running. She picked it up and again began to run till she went out of the building and I lost her view. I came back into my room and lay on the floor.

I was lying down when the door opened. I opened my eyes to see who was at the door and saw Aarohi's other half with darkness over her shoulders where her head was supposed to be.

'What is with this odor? Did someone come here?' Aarohi's other half asked in a suspicious tone.

'No. No one came here. Your are the first person I am meeting today.' I lied.

'I won't believe you. I am sure someone was here before me. Tell me you scum, who was here? Was it Aarohi?' She grabbed my neck and pressed it with such force.

'I am telling you the truth. No one came here. Please trust me.' I tried to speak, but she just ignored my broken words. In no time, my face turned red with the lack of oxygen. Out of nowhere, she pulled a knife from her pocket and held it against my neck.

'If you want to live, tell me the truth. Tell me who was here before me? Was it that bitch Aarohi?' I could see the rage all over her face.

'No. No one was here. Please don't…' I tried to speak, but before I could complete my sentence, she slit my neck with the knife. I could feel the blood dripping out of my neck. 'Please don't do this. I can't take it anymore. Please leave me alone. PLEASE….' I screamed. Suddenly, I heard a man's voice calling out my name.

'Wake up. Someone came to see you. WAKE UP,' the man shouted. His sharp voice went into my ears and made me uneasy. I opened my eyes partially, and in my blurred vision, I saw Tihar jail's cell where I was locked up. The man kept striking his wooden rod on the bars of the iron gate. The sound came when the wooden rod hitting on the iron gate stung in my ears and helped me return to reality. 'Wake up. A girl is waiting to meet you. Hurry up.'

'I am up, can't you see? Who has come to meet me? What is the girl's name?' I asked while rubbing my eyes.

'I don't know. You only have ten minutes together. Whatever you want to talk about or want to do, finish it in ten minutes.' The guard gave a weird smile and left. After he went, I stood up to pee. I heard someone calling my name.

'Hello, Pranav? How are you? I hope you are doing great in here.' Standing next to the main gate Kirti began to laugh hysterically.

'I will kill you, bitch.' I shouted and ran toward her. Just as I reached her, she pulled a pen out of her hair bun and pointed it toward me.

'If you take one more step toward me, then I will bury this pen into your eyeball.' She threatened me. Looking at her face, I realized she is serious and will do what she is saying. I went back inside my room and sat on the floor. Kirti followed me and sat on the floor at some distance from me, which made her feel safe.

'Why have you come here? Aren't you satisfied with what you did to me? I asked and tried not to look into her eyes.

'Just wanted to see how badly you were suffering. Now you can feel Aarohi's pain?'

'I never wanted anything to happen to her. If you have read Aarohi's journal, then you must know I loved her the most in my life. Whatever happened between us, happened because of the other Pranav. Why did God make me this way?' I cried out loud.

'That is not an excuse for what you did. If you knew you had some issues, then why did you come into a relationship with Aarohi in the first place?'

'I loved her with all of my heart. I fell in love with her the moment I saw her. At the time I thought the other Pranav also liked Aarohi and would not make her suffer as he had done earlier with my girlfriends. But I was wrong. If I had known the things would repeat, I would have never dated her in the first place.'

'This is of no use talking about the past. It doesn't make any sense now. The guard told me it's your hanging day tomorrow. If you have any last wish, you can tell me now. I promise you I will make sure to fulfill your wish.'

'No. I don't have any wishes. I am just happy that I will die tomorrow. Finally, everything will stop, and I will be free from this pathetic life.'

'Fine, if you feel that way. But I would like to help you a little, even if you want or not. Here, take this. This is rat poison. If you don't want to go through all the pain and humiliation, then drink it. You will be dead in no time. You will get the best possible pain-free death.' Kirti handed me a small packet filled with powder of rat poison.

'Why are you helping me? What I did to your cousin is unforgivable, but still, you are helping me. Why?' I asked in amazement.

'After all these years, you still didn't understand me. Mr. Pranav Sharma, I still love you. I loved you and will love you in the coming future, no matter what. My love for you is endless. Remember this till your last breath. I have to go now. Goodbye Pranav.' Kirti stood up and went out of the cell. After she left, I kept staring at the packet of poison for a few minutes, trying to decide what to do with it. Finally, I opened it and swallowed the entire packet, and drank some sips of water to gulp it down. For a few minutes, nothing happened, but then suddenly, my head began to spin, and I felt like vomiting. White foam started to flow out of my mouth. I faltered a little and, while losing control over my body, I collapsed on the floor.

A few minutes passed, and I felt an emptiness inside me. But then suddenly I felt something. I tried to open my eyes to see where I am but failed. After many unsuccessful attempts, finally, I opened my eyes partially and saw darkness all around me. I tried to move my body but was not able to. I felt like I went paralyzed, and was only able to roll my eyes. Just then, I heard the sound of someone's footsteps approaching me. I tried to find the voice source but didn't able to do so. A few seconds later, a girl came out from the darkness and stood in front of me. I rolled my eyes toward her and when I analyzed her body, I only found her lower half till her shoulders. She didn't have her head and in place of it, I saw nothing other than darkness.

'How are you, Pranav? Did she hurt you?' the girl asked while sitting next to me.

'Aarohi, is that you? I recognize your voice. My love, My Aarohi.'

'So finally, you know what my voice sounds like. I am happy to know that. Tell me about the cut on your neck. Does it hurt?'

'What cut? I don't have any cuts.' I said with amazement.

'My other half gave you a cut when she got to know that I came to meet you in your cell. But now, we don't need to get scared of her anymore. I took care of her.'

'What? What do you mean? What did you do to her?' I asked.

'I killed her. When she tried to hurt you, something inside me got triggered, and I did what I had to.' Just when she completed her sentence, blood began to flow from the cut on my neck. Aarohi tried to stop it, but the cut was very deep. Losing so much blood made me dizzy. I felt like my soul was trying to escape through the severe cut which Aarohi's other half gave me.

'Baby, I think I am dying. I will not survive this,' I said in broken words.

'No, baby. Don't say that. I won't let you die.' Aarohi pulled out a knife from her jeans pocket. With the help of the blade, she cut her wrist, and a stream of blood began to flow from it. She placed her wrist on my lips, and the drops of blood started falling into my mouth. Every drop of blood was giving me a new life. Those drops are not just blood. For me, they were drops of life. A few minutes later, Aarohi collapsed on the floor next to me. To get a look at what happened to her, I tried to move my body, and this time I was able to. With the help of my hands, I placed Aarohi's body over my lap and looked at her face. There I saw nothing other than darkness. Looking at her not moving, tears began to roll out of my eyes. In no time, I began to mourn.

Still feeling a little dazed, I heard someone shout, 'It is an emergency. Give us the way. Please give us a way to move the stretcher.' I tried to open my eyes to what was happening around me. With a bit of effort, I opened my eyes partially and saw the hospital's moving ceiling. Some men from the hospital staff took me to the ICU room and finally shifted me to the ICU bed. As soon as they placed me in the ICU, someone gave me an injection. The injection made me dizzy, and I lost my consciousness.

'Wake up. How are you, Pranav? Tell me, how are you feeling? I heard a lady's voice asking me questions.

'I am fine…' I mumbled, but my broken words didn't make much sense to her.

'Pranav, you are safe now. We have given you an antidote for the poison that you took. You are out of danger now. Do you understand what I am saying?' I opened my mouth to reply to her but failed as I was still under the anesthesia effect and couldn't feel my body. So, I nodded my head to say that I understand.

'Okay. That is such great news. Now I am going to give you your medicine. Open your mouth, Pranav. Say Aaaa…' said the lady doctor. Listening to her, I opened my mouth, and she dropped a tablet inside my mouth. She made me drink some water. The water helped and with ease I gulped the tablet inside.

'Listen Pranav, now I am going to check on some other patients. They also need proper supervision like you. Right? So, if you need anything, then just ring this bell. Someone will be here to help you,' the lady said while pointing to the bell and turned to leave the room. I tried to open my eyes to see whom I was talking to. With a little struggle, I opened my eyes, but she had already turned around to leave. I caught a glimpse of the golden bracelet that she was wearing. It was exactly like the one I saw on Aarohi's wrist in my dream. I was aghast and I blacked out.